The Exene Chronicles

The Exene Chronicles

CAMILLE A. COLLINS

KINDRED BOOKS
GREEN BAY, WISCONSIN

Published in the United States by Kindred Books, an imprint of Brain Mill Press.
Print ISBN 978-1-948559-05-8
EPUB ISBN 978-1-948559-06-5
MOBI ISBN 978-1-948559-07-2
PDF ISBN 978-1-948559-08-9

Cover art by Crystal White.
Cover design by Danikqwa Rambert.

www.theexenechronicles.com

"You don't need to write a novel
if you feel at home in the world."
—Andrea Barrett

An Angel, A Radiant Star

C o n t e n t s

The Exene Chronicles

Inflorescent Tears

IT WAS NOT THE PAPER DOLL CUTOUT, BUT EXENE'S actual mouth that Lia imagined, twisted into a snarl, blaming her. *'It's you, Lia! It's all your fault what happened to Ryan!'* Because Lia's mother had woken her to say Ryan never made it home the previous night. Fraught with worry, Mrs. Green had already phoned the police, and Lia's first thought was that Ryan must be dead.

Right away, Lia found the only way to deal with the worst possible scenario was to confront it head-on, to embrace it as though she were cradling in her arms a soft kitten. Lia's rendition of the death of her very best friend was not especially morbid, or as gruesomely detailed as it might have been. It was the quixotic rendering of a burgeoning poetess.

At the very least, Ryan deserved the grandeur of theater. So Lia envisioned the most enchanted garden, a neat little knoll of green, green grass nestled beneath an elegant magnolia tree in full bloom. That graceful magnolia would weep its ripe, inflorescent tears down onto a grand mausoleum. Ryan's body would lie inside, near the hollow mouth of her final abode, a structure built of the finest marble, festooned with chiseled hearts, and inside those hearts would be inscribed eternal valentines proclaiming, *"Ryan we love you"* and *"Forever in our hearts,"* all with floating cupids, their arrows shooting heavenward. Ryan's body would lie cold, her skin luminous, enlivened by the candent glow of four flaming torches, bathing her heart-shaped face in a delicate nimbus of pale yellow light. Her body would be covered by a white linen sheet, and nestled against the slope of her shoulders and the tapering silhouette of her waist and legs would be flowers: orchids and white roses, failing in all their beauty to compare to Ryan's infinitely ravishing, cold, dead grace.

Lia's short reverie was disturbed by her mother's persistence—Mrs. Payne stood in the doorway of Lia's bedroom with a hand on her hip. "Baby, you've got to get up. Don't be scared now. The police just want to talk to you about what you and Ryan did last night."

the vanity
of tiny shoes

RIGHT BEFORE HER DISAPPEARING ACT, RYAN HAD finally blossomed. With the help of ninety-nine cents worth of drugstore peroxide, she had transformed from a brunette with a head full of muted brown hair to a blonde possessed of the sort of ravishing, buxom beauty of almost another era. For there was something very film noir, a dollop of some essence teetering toward the burlesque about her—like a young Monroe. Unfortunately for Ryan, her particular look did not draw a parallel to a Marilyn of fifteen or sixteen; Ryan was an approximate, though more tender, prototype of Ms. Monroe at middle age, when her figure had stretched beyond the voluptuous to a form slightly more grotesque.

This strange beauty of Ryan's—her husky voice, her height (from the ages of eleven to thirteen, she had shot from 5' 3" to 5' 9"), her quaking limbs, large hands, and heaving bust—gave her a grand and dramatic beauty wholly unsuitable for a girl in a Southern California middle school. The young boys her own age were singularly intrigued yet frightened and repulsed by the sight of her, striding down the hallways at school all Viking and grandiose, while older men simply couldn't get enough of her. The sole arrow that pointed to any girlish charm was her face: young, heart-shaped, pale, and baby plump: the mien of some milkmaid in a nineteenth-century painting.

Ryan set everyone at ease with her affable babysitter charm. Yet beneath her sunny, unblemished exterior, there brewed an intensity, a profound impatience with the purgatory of adolescence. Striding around the Baxter family master bedroom, a rogue babysitter in a pair of Mrs. Baxter's pumps, the mistress's black negligee pulled tight over her ample body, Ryan laughed and tossed her head back and rolled about the bed in a fit of giggles. Lia stood by, remonstrating with her like a stern parent. "Ryan, stop it! The Baxters will be home any minute and you'll wake the kids."

Lia and Ryan's inseparability formed of near necessity, as grand things sometimes do. Ryan, who at eleven had been menstruating and wearing bras before every other girl in her class, was something of an outcast. Lia, small and wide-eyed and pretty to everyone except herself, was one of about only five black kids in the entire middle and high schools combined. Both were somewhat withdrawn and more in love with the dreams floating inside their heads than social obligations that demanded perfectly blow-dried hair.

... because
sometimes even Jimi Hendrix
was the odd man out

CORONADO, ADRIFT IN THE MIDST OF SAN DIEGO BAY, that lone puzzle piece tucked beneath the sofa cushion that becomes a small puzzle unto itself.

Lia was the only dollop of chocolate in a row of blondes and a token brunette on the beach, the afternoon sun hanging low above the lazy, slow-moving waves. She squirmed in her bikini when Megan Hamilton declared, "I'm practically nigger on my belly from laying out all day." Terror ripped through Lia's small frame, preempting anger, quivering from her small feet and shooting straight to her brain like a bullet. It was the fear of the social isolation she'd face if she stood up and stomped Megan in the face like she wanted. Instead, she slyly kicked a small mound of sand onto the corner of Megan's towel.

The other girls yawned with insouciance, stretching their tawny limbs and wondering what to eat for lunch.

Taking a deep breath, Lia tried to calm herself. They were her friends; they liked her. Yet she was expected to consume the racist epithets that glided off Megan's sassy tongue in the same way that the waves felt themselves powerless to keep from tumbling toward the shore. Alternately, she could simply choose not to have any friends at all. What did it matter? Before long she'd find herself lying on her towel all alone while the others frolicked in the ocean because getting her permed hair wet was a whole other thing.

She had a love-hate relationship with *Different Strokes*. She took comfort in the sight of other black faces like hers, plus the older boy Willis was pretty cute. But she detested the fawning, eager condescension of Mr. Drummond and his perky daughter Kimberly, and most of all, she hated the way the little boy Arnold— whose part was played by an actor who in real life was older than she was—bugged his eyes out, pursed his lips, and said, *"Whatcha talkin' bout Willis?"* on every single episode. She did not know Stepin Fetchit, and she was only vaguely familiar with Amos 'n' Andy— she only knew she hated when the little boy started in with his entertaining little darky routine.

Things got better when Janet Jackson came on the show to play the girlfriend of the handsome boy Willis, because at least she was pretty and wore her hair cute and wasn't being abused or crying all the time like when she played Penny on *Good Times*.

"LET'S GO BACK FOR A MOMENT TO THIS NEIL. YOU SAY he lives in Imperial Beach?" Lia had not imagined that the police made house calls. She'd envisioned a more chilling scene. She imagined being escorted into a sparse chamber with a metal table and chairs to be questioned for hours under a harsh light.

Propped between her parents on the sofa, she felt like a child. The officer's skin was an odd combination of beige and orange tones from excessive parlor tanning. In his early forties, his flesh spread generously over his massive frame. All the while, as he sat on the sofa opposite the Payne family, Lia's eyes kept drifting to his lavishly dense fingers. It seemed to her that they were fingers suffering from misuse. Hands not meant for pulling pistol triggers or handcuffing illegal aliens, but thick, soft tools better suited to more tactile pursuits, like kneading dough or chiseling the alphabet onto baby's blocks.

For Lia, nothing the police officer said could redeem the situation from its patent absurdity. A meeting taken at the police station would have made the dilemma seem more real. As it was, Lia could only fume quietly, furious with Ryan for leaving her holding the bag, for getting her into trouble while she suddenly slipped behind a curtain of mystery. Perhaps it was normal for a girl, not yet fifteen, to approach the situation with a certain stubborn obtuseness, for in the sage retrospect of a few hours, Lia had come to realize the grim fears she'd felt after initially being told about Ryan were nothing but hyperbole, paranoia.

Hadn't there been a kidnapping? A small child spirited away just the previous summer from the park just blocks away? No. Lia shook the thought from her head. It was totally different with little kids. Who would try and make off with Ryan? Ryan, who was mistaken in restaurants and shopping malls for a grown woman (department store clerks often asked if she wanted to establish a line of credit).

Lia also hadn't thought that police officers, like secretaries, scribbled notes onto little blocks of paper. He looked absurd, perched on the edge of the sofa, his thighs nearly bursting like the Incredible Hulk's through the close weft of his beige trousers.

"So, this Neil, you ever been over to his place with Ryan?"

"No." Lia shook her head resolutely. The penetration of her parents' eyes, both sets upon her, was both subtle and intense, so that their collective, boring gaze swelled to a thin murmur. Their unrelenting stares actually made a sound, like the low, throaty growl of some forest-dwelling rodent.

"You sure now?" The police officer gently nudged her toward a confession. Lacking even the slightest measure of Ryan's defiance, Lia easily capitulated.

"Well, now that I think of it, I might have been there for a little while, but only one time for sure."

Lia's mother gasped and looked sharply at the officer. "You mean this man had these girls over to his house? Good lord. Officer, how old did you say he was?"

Lia wished she could stuff a wad of paper towels inside her mother's throat. The officer had already said Neil was twenty-one. Yet turning to face Lia's father, Greg, Dorothea Payne was still incredulous. "I can't believe anyone so bold. A grown man keeping company with girls just out of middle school!"

Lia writhed in her spot, her mother's words like knives, stabbing her repeatedly. By attacking Neil, her mother indirectly made her feel filthy. They'd only watched *Starsky and Hutch* and a rerun of *Dallas* and eaten tacos. That was all. Besides, he was Ryan's boyfriend, not hers.

"Umm." The police officer paused to mull over this fact. "Where did you, or Ryan, say you met this fellow, Neil?"

"I didn't meet him anywhere. Ryan did!" Lia blurted her words at the officer angrily. She could feel the penetration of her mother's eyes, glaring with the suggestion that Lia change her tone. She couldn't win.

Her mother suspected the worst, and yet Lia had to speak respectfully as the officer insinuated things with his probing questions.

"Okay, Lia, you're doing great. I've just got one more question. This may be a little uncomfortable for you, but it's important."

Here, the officer paused to moisten his lips with a rapid flick of his tongue. Lia couldn't be certain of what the officer would ask next, but she had an idea and thus could feel herself cringing as he began to speak.

"Did Neil ever touch you, or speak to you in a sexual way? Did he ever try to coax you into any sort of sexual act, either he or any of his friends?"

This time, it may have been Lia who gasped audibly, or at least she thought she had. Never had she been so humiliated. Her parents at either side stared silently, impatiently awaiting her answer.

"No! Never!" This time, she felt her impertinent tone completely justified and didn't care whether her mother liked it or not. Lia refused to lift her gaze to entertain her mother's possible glare, or worse yet, an irritating look of relief spread across her face.

"You sure now? There's nothing to be embarrassed about if he tried anything. It wouldn't be your fault..." With the officer adding to her humiliation with every syllable he uttered, Lia spoke no words and only responded with a firm look that said she had nothing more to offer on the subject.

"All righty." The officer stood in a surprisingly agile motion. "With these types of situations, the first week or so is crucial. I hate to be the one to sound grim, but beyond that, it might be weeks or months before we ever figure out what's happened. Anyway, here's my card." The officer bent to look Lia in the eye and offer her a plastic smile. "Please give me a call if you think of any new information that might help us locate your friend, okay?"

Lia—perched on the sofa tearing tissue in her hands, still shaken by the officer's questions and angry that Ryan had abandoned her—felt winded, as though someone had taken a fist to her stomach. She watched, though, as her father thanked the officer for his time and extended his large brown hand for a handshake. It seemed the officer, who had been quite patient and friendly in questioning her, grasped her father's hand with reluctance.

At the open front door, the officer halted, and as he turned toward Greg Payne, Lia thought sure that his once open and friendly face had become clouded with an intense look, of fear or malevolence perhaps, and she couldn't be certain if he was just shielding his eyes from a stream of sunlight angling through the door or what, because for some reason his expression had changed, his eyes narrowed down to thin slots where one might fit a coin.

"So, you folks own or rent?" The officer blocked the doorway, unwilling to move until his question was answered.

"Beg pardon?" Lia could see her father's jaw harden, taking on the telltale clench that suggested his irritation.

"Just curious how long you folks have been here."

"About two years now." Lia noted that her father strained to keep his upbeat tone.

"Two years, eh? How long do you plan to stay?"

Lia couldn't understand what was happening. The faint shifts in the atmosphere of the Payne living room were real, yet surreal at the same time. She was surprised that the same officer now sounded rude, like one of those surfers who came to class stoned without as much as a notebook and was quick to smart off to the teacher.

"Well, I don't know. I'd say we're pretty happy, pretty well settled right now." Lia noticed that her father spoke loudly, in a formal tone. It was the voice he reserved for important telephone calls and tactful quarrels with restaurant managers when there was some discrepancy with the bill.

To Greg Payne's reply, the officer only snorted with open incredulity as he carried his hulking frame down the porch steps.

Lia worried about the possibility of further proceedings, if in time she'd be asked to testify under oath or take a lie detector test. She felt burdened by the woe of unspoken truths, for when asked about Neil's friends, she'd purposefully neglected to mention the sailor Keith, a man (Had he been twenty-one or twenty-two? She couldn't remember.) whom she'd kissed, and who she wished was available to spirit her away just as Neil had taken off in his Camaro with Ryan on so many balmy summer nights.

It seemed to Lia that if they'd only stop wasting time with questioning and talk, they'd find Ryan watching television at the condo at The Cays with Neil or sprawled out beside him on those white patio chairs next to the pool, lulled to sleep by the heat of the afternoon sun.

Cobblestones, crisscrossed by scarlet rills...

Away from the clean, wide streets of Coronado, downtown San Diego, with its vagrant hotels, Salvation Army treasures, and errant trash tumbling along the gutters, provided Ryan and Lia some undefined relief. The grit egged on their teething pathos, their emerging view of life through some inverted prism, where on the one hand, they believed that in some far-off distance they would attain a sort of middle-class contentment, but for the present, nothing besides a noncommittal flirtation with the dark, baneful, and untoward, procured in the pedestrian way of most fourteen-year-olds (through books, music, and imaginative musings), could create for them a sense of satisfaction.

In order to feed their insatiable quest for all things bleak on a diet more substantial than what Danielle Steel had to offer, the girls' eighth grade English teacher introduced them to Baudelaire. Whether or not they had really understood *The Fountain of Blood* was hard to say.

"*Romeo and Juliet* isn't so melodramatic," Ryan murmured reflectively.

"I mean, who wouldn't die for love? I would…if it came to that."

"You're nuts."

"It's just…I think that Prince song is right: the party's over in the year 2000. Do you realize we'll be, like, thirty years old, if we even live to see 2000?"

"Wait. What's that got to do with anything?" Lia frowned.

"I dunno, it's just…I'd rather die young for love instead of living without it, not knowing what might happen. Have you ever seen those warships down at the end of Palm Avenue? I hate them."

Lia paused to consider Ryan's words.

"You're right. I never thought about it that way…but you're absolutely right. I guess I'd prefer it that way too."

Apparently, what Mrs. Buchanan had offered as a cautionary tale had suffered gross misinterpretation.

With the endless choices of the Salvation Army thrift store came the opportunity to take on whatever costume, and with it, whichever fantasy role they chose. Much like their descendant courtship with melancholy, their love of the clothes and hairstyles of the late 1950s and early '60s was not grounded in reality, but in the promise of some Shangri-la where girls beguiled with hooded eyelids and teased hair, the glimmer of pale, iridescent gloss on full lips.

"Lia! You've got to see what I found for you!"

Ryan gave up waiting and raced to the back of the store, where Lia was admiring jewel-encrusted pocketbooks, and grabbed her by the hand. In a row of old frocks, some of them musty and stained, others absurd in their grandiose embellishment of floor-length drapery, puffed sleeve, and sequin, Ryan had discovered a jewel.

"Stand still now." Taking her by the shoulders, Ryan made Lia stand tall and straight while she held the sleeveless, pink satin, '60s-style dress up to Lia's small frame.

Stepping in front of a mirror with the dress draped against her body, Lia cried, "Oh my god. I love it! I can't believe how rad you are!" She threw her arms around Ryan's neck.

"It'll be your Supremes dress," Ryan decided.

Ryan wasn't as lucky in finding anything special at the thrift shop that day. To strike out at the Salvation Army was one thing, but at the drugstore there was never any shortage of items for consolation. With exactly $8.37 worth of merchandise between them, the girls were delighted by the prospect of getting back home where, imprisoned inside their still girlishly furnished bedrooms turned out in fluffy white comforters and stuffed unicorns, which they clung to during witching hours, when they dreamt of being spirited away by those creatures come to life, they would work up their sadness like warm palms dredging up the dark forces of a Ouija Board.

As they clambered onto the bus that would take them back to their serene pocket of suburbia, the two girls clasped hands.

"I love you!" Lia squealed. "You're my best friend in the entire world!"

"You're mine too!" Ryan cried.

If spilling peroxide on the pale green bathroom rug, which caused a spreading white stain and made Ryan's mom yell at the girls, wasn't foreshadowing—a telling clue that all that conjuring had been unnecessary— then Ryan's cocky attitude once the peroxide took hold, and she showed up to school the next day tossing her long blond hair all over the place, should have been.

"Coming over after school?" Lia leaned over to whisper as they prepped for a science lab.

Ryan shook her head. "Elizabeth Cole's sneaking boys over while her mom's out. I'd invite you, but you don't drink, don't make out..." Ryan flung her hair off her shoulder and abruptly turned away.

Ryan's introduction to Neil Jimenez two weeks later wasn't exactly the dream prescribed by the clutching of those unicorns, or their infant attachment to Baudelaire's feverish lamentations; neither was the fact that Lia would end up donning her pretty pink "Supremes" dress on the loneliest day of her life.

"... We're Desperate Get used to It." —X

Ryan remembered smashing the antique lantern in the catalytic moment that drove her family out west. She had never been a tidy, picturesque type of little girl, but was always chubby and a bit disheveled, with wisps of hair hanging all around her face and falling into her eyes.

"It was an accident. I'm sorry, Mommy." Ryan buried her guilty face into small, plump hands, white knee socks soiled with dirt and sunken down around her ankles. Her lavender polyester dress—a frock one of the Brady girls might have worn—stretched tight around her belly.

Karen Green hunched over the coffee table chain smoking, her face bruised with dark emotion. She couldn't have cared less about the lamp. "So long as you haven't cut yourself, sweetie," she muttered. She stashed the bottle of gin beneath the table, taking aimless swigs when Ryan's head was turned. Drinking in broad daylight in front of a first grader felt wrong—unseemly.

"Never mind the lamp, just go and get yourself a dolly to play with," she whispered before crashing face-first onto the couch drunk. The neighbors in their modest apartment complex smelled smoke and called the fire department.

Karen Green, morose and worked over at twenty-eight by fatigue, the taste of dissatisfaction thick inside her mouth. Exhausted by the fact that whatever was supposed to have happened—the culmination of some unspoken dream—never had.

She *had* lived her dream of being a stewardess, sort of. She'd never flown to Paris, Milan, or even New York. For some reason her supervisor always selected her for the domestic, Midwestern shifts. Minneapolis to Chicago, Milwaukee to St. Louis. Instead of a handsome pilot with whom to fall in love, she was routinely paired with Mr. James, a belligerent captain. She'd met Bruce, a computer technician, and had been three months pregnant with Ryan on her wedding day, and that had been that.

In the way children filter and store odd tidbits of old wives' tales and garbled information, cobbling together their own encyclopedias of knowledge, Ryan believed coffee was good for a variety of things, including the revival of a mother passed out on the sofa at 1 p.m. She'd fiddled with the stove and a tea towel caught fire. Too panicked to move, she watched—a plump and well-meaning little girl, both haunted and seduced by the flames illuminating her face. The paramedics busted through the door and carried Ryan and Karen to safety.

For a time, Bruce Green had applied himself, stroking Karen's hair in the hospital, where they'd kept her and Ryan under observation for smoke inhalation. Recklessly, like diamonds after a fight, Bruce proffered California. They'd discussed it before, but now was the time to go. Sunshine, beaches; they'd teach their kids to surf. California might be her last shot—at glamour, adventure, the acquisition of some vague success, Karen reckoned dimly at the time. Out of the hospital and sober for a week, *"We're moving out west,"* she announced triumphantly at the salon as the girl filed her nails. Similar declarations were made at church on Sunday and over the telephone to sisters, cousins, and friends.

In the end, it had been just what they'd called it and nothing more. A move. A change of geographic location. Ungirded, removed from extended family gatherings and potluck suppers at church—in some way, things simply got worse. The Greens were not wealthy; they were neither tanned nor thin. They did not own tennis rackets or move in the type of circle that brunched at the Hotel Del or went sailing at the weekend. Their California dream: so close at hand, yet impossibly out of reach.

In 1975, Ryan Green broke a lantern in Palatine, Illinois. Long before Christie Brinkley ever appeared on the cover of *Cosmopolitan* in a high-cut swimsuit, Ryan knew she had failed. In the seven minutes it had taken for the firemen and paramedics to arrive, she'd gathered new data and collected new facts for her encyclopedia.

"Keep your electric eye on me babe..."
—moonage daydream

RONNIE SPECTOR: There's nothing new under the sun, babe. Punk, smunk. I mean, can you even sing a note a cappella?

EXENE CERVENKA: How many of your own lyrics did you say you ever wrote? What's that? Yeah. Thought so.

"Dropping the phone she leaves it dead to the dead men. Heat is the point, smoke on the receiver. Light up to its universal ringing. Like a woman." —X

THESE ARE THE WORDS THAT LIA AND RYAN SING ONE afternoon when they sit and listen to X. Their tender voices rising, they sing loudly and off-key at a passionate treble, and for a moment, the inhibition of speaking up in class, trying out for cheerleading, or changing for gym not openly, but hidden behind a locker—*dissipates*.

Ryan thrashes her head from side to side, swinging her arms about wildly, pausing only to turn to Lia and say, "This album is so rad!"

Lia sits still, quiet and pensive, but she is taking it in. Her attitude is more jazz than punk. She is kick-back relaxed, serene, chill, yet concentrated on every nuance rising off the turntable. An elite lyrical connoisseur, she nods her head slowly and gives a silent nod of approval that is worth its weight in syllables.

In their initial days together, when the skies were colored by the incandescent blush of easy sunsets, the girls spent many afternoons in the record shop in San Diego where they felt grown up (though they sometimes pretended they were in the King's Road). They made weekly pilgrimages, eager to splurge pocket money on albums by The Specials, Madness, and Sex Pistols.

With an insatiable hunger for the next new thing, they spied a unique record, the cover brandishing a broad, thick letter X shimmering in gold foil. The album's title, *Wild Gift*, seemed suitably apropos; the girls were ever on a quest for the gift of new adventure. They pulled the album from the racks, intrigued: a band named succinctly after one odd, infrequently used letter of the alphabet.

On the back of the album was a photograph of four young musicians, a girl and three good-looking guys (but the one they will later discover the girl is married to is the handsomest one of all). The girl bears the look of a wild barmaid, a starlet of some perpetual nighttime, with an assurance, a confident gaze—the type of girl who would never be shamed by losing a catfight. A girl, it seemed, with many wry bons mots poised to fire off the tip of her tongue.

The girls selected the album without even asking the clerk to spin them a tune, trusting somehow that it would meet their expectation: flippant, sad, clever, and enraged sounds streaming from the throat of the intense-looking girl with a mouth frowned by a sullen defiance.

Like an infant pet, they carried the record home gingerly, anxious to see how well this new band would integrate itself into their lives. In Ryan's living room, they switched on the stereo, reverentially sipping cans of generic black cherry soda from the Safeway, as though attending a christening of something brand-new and possibly precious.

Music seeped through the speakers and *pow!* The moment the disc began to spin on the turntable, it was magic; a sound fast, thrashing, melodic, ripped through the speakers like lightning, like fire. The girls listened carefully, not wanting to miss a single riff. They were instantly captivated by the girl singer Exene's sometimes mournful, sometimes furiously invincible wail, and the surprisingly sweet harmony of her and John Doe singing together.

Many of the songs began in a flurry; the gates open on a racetrack and the horses fly! Played fast and ending abruptly with the slam of a door that gives finality to an argument, the notes standing on tiptoe. With a final crash of D.J. Bonebrake's symbol or a shrill note of Billy Zoom's guitar, it was over; the band had done its job, transporting the girls to a new place and finishing off each song, each one a little universe theretofore unknown—sharp and matter of fact when it was over.

RYAN'S BROTHER, JEFF, WAS TWO YEARS HER SENIOR. He was pale, thin, and narrow-shouldered. He and his friends spent most of their time indoors reading comic books and sharing jokes that expressed a crude sexuality of which they had no firsthand experience, whereas most boys their age had abandoned such pursuits years before.

Only thirteen, and damned with the heaving bust of a duchess, Ryan padded down the hallway to her bedroom in bare feet after a shower, startled from a daydream by the sound of boys galloping after her. As though some fever of puberty had made them crazed, all three took advantage of the absence of Mr. and Mrs. Green, sticking index fingers into the dimples of Ryan's thighs, tickling the marshmallow flesh that oozed irresistibly over the upper edge of her towel.

"You're such the porker, Ryan. Why don't you take your butt out for a walk sometime?" They taunted with cruel words, yet their delighted fingertips told a different story.

In an instant, the situation turned frightening. They hadn't meant to pull her towel down, only to tease her baby fat and mock her nakedness.

In the confusion of the boys' sharp, grotesque laughter—of their fast, groping hands and balled fists which they used to beat against her bare arms and calves until they were red and blotchy—the towel fell a few inches and Ryan was left to weep and cower in a corner of the hallway.

"Please! Please stop doing that to me!" she sobbed. Jeff finally masked his sister's shame with the wet towel, escorting her by the elbow to her room. The others backed away frightened, their eyes unaverted.

an angel, a radiant star

"YOU'RE SO CAREFUL WITH THE SCISSORS. I DON'T have that kind of patience. Just tear it, see?" Ryan ripped a photo of Siouxsie Sioux out of an old copy of *Rolling Stone*. The girls had felt quite grand, pooling their babysitting cash and having Lia's father write them a check for the subscription. The old copies worked perfectly for the collages. Their months of handiwork lay stashed beneath Lia's bed in a thick folder.

One afternoon, Ryan had casually cut up a couple of old family pictures and aimlessly pasted the faces of her mother, father, and brother onto photos of random things, a telephone pole or the body of a horse. Only Lia had a hard time accepting such an odd, slightly disturbing act as the "joke" Ryan named it in order to minimize the scandalized shriek Lia emitted as she watched Ryan take a scissors to the snapshots.

"Ryan! Are you crazy? That's so morbid!"

"I'm entitled to my rage, Lia. Every day, I tell them how hard it is, gooney football players staring at my chest and whispering like dorks. Even Mr. Brown, that creep. He just stared at me when I went up after class to ask him about the homework. It was like I wasn't even human, like there was nothing going on with me above the neck."

Ryan moved her hands swiftly as she spoke, as though she had to work fast in order to control her swelling anger. "Every time, they say the same thing. *'Oh, honey. It's just a rough phase. Ignore those boys; they're just immature and stupid. Besides, it's normal. Lots of girls go through this type of thing, not just you.'* Well, who says it's normal? What makes them think they have the right? You'd think my own parents would take my side."

Lia couldn't really argue with Ryan's impassioned defense. She simply looked on quietly as Ryan applied dark ink to her cutouts, blackening her parents' eyes and scratching angry words across their thin paper chests as though they were wearing sloganed T-shirts. *"Traitor!"* Or, *"I suck!"* The words seemed to scream. Sometimes Ryan even fashioned little cardboard coffins out of scissors and glue and sent them to an early grave.

Lia came up with the more jovial idea of casting themselves in party scenes. Here was a swivel-headed Lia at a New York fete with Annabella Lwin. There was Ryan, standing shoulder to shoulder with Debbie Harry and Patti Smith backstage after a concert in London.

"Noel Redding is like this crazy red-haired guitarist. Anyway, sometimes he and the drummer, you know, for the Hendrix Experience, used to gang up on Jimi. They called him a nigger even." Lia breathlessly related this newly gleaned information.

"That's crazy. I mean, he was, like, *Jimi Hendrix...*" Ryan reflected as she smeared glue onto the back of the picture of Siouxsie Sioux.

"I know. Even *he* had to put up with crap." Lia sighed. "I wish there was no school tomorrow. I just want to stay home and finish this collage, or run away to England." And yet, The Clash played on in the background, and it was as if the Coronado Bridge linked directly to the Tower Bridge in London and birthed them unto the world, the mauling rhythms of punk a golden ring in the mouth of a dark horse.

Lady Luck

THEY PACKED A PICNIC LUNCH, BUT IT WAS HOT AND they couldn't be bothered to walk all the way over to Balboa Park, so they settled for the nearest bus stop instead. They snapped off the tabs on their diet cream sodas and each swallowed one diet pill pilfered from Mrs. Green's stash. They threw away the ham sandwiches and all but four of the orange slices Mrs. Green had packed for them, but devoured the packet of Twinkies she'd sent along for them to share, and then complained to one another of wretched hunger and light-headedness all day long.

They sat on the bus stop bench, relishing the shade of the bus shelter as cars and buses moved along the avenue.

"I told my mom the most ridiculous, convoluted lie!" Ryan snorted. "I said we were going over to San Diego to pick up one of Crazy Margaret's cats from the vet, and then we'd bring the cat back in a carrier on the bus and wait with it until she got in from a date with her old black boyfriend, Spanks!" Ryan's face went red and she gasped and sputtered, diet cream soda spurting from the sides of her mouth, she laughed so hard. Lia tittered with uncertainty, tickled by an imagined vision of Crazy Margaret and this boyfriend–some old smooth talker, Spanks. Yet she felt an unease, not knowing exactly what part of the fib Ryan found so funny.

Parents had strange, sometimes contradictory rules. Lia was allowed to go unchaperoned to concerts, to see bands like Black Flag thrash it out live and in person, but when she guilelessly told her mother the title of the R-rated documentary *The Decline of Western Civilization*, freely speaking her intention to watch bands like X and The Germs play songs and talk about punk, the plan was shot down with a resounding "No!"

"I don't even like the sound of that," her mother had said. *"Besides, you're underage, and I'm certainly not going along and sit through that mess."* Of course, Lia's mom had no real knowledge of Black Flag or what kind of music they played. If anything, the idea of a charming evening at a concert sounded cultured to her.

"But why didn't you just tell her the truth? I thought you said your mom didn't care?"

"She doesn't, but I'm playing it safe. Because what if your mom calls and asks? If your mom finds out and gets mad, we'll be in just as much trouble."

These were the days when Ryan acted as a leader, a true friend who thought things through and covered for her.

Getting tickets for the film had required some scheming. "The only way we're going to get in is on Sunday, the late show," Lia had whispered during History. "Jesse's boyfriend, Hector, works at the theater. He's already seventeen. He said we have to get our tickets early in the afternoon, when his boss is on break, then come back at 10 p.m. after the boss goes home. We've got to play it cool, he said, and carry ourselves like much older girls. We can't hang around acting gooney or he'll get busted. We'll dress older and put on lots of makeup on the bus ride over." It was an unusual role for Lia, being in charge, but the movie theater connection came through Jesse, her friend.

"What are we going to do for all those hours?" Ryan had pondered, stretched out on her side on the phone in her bedroom, loving every minute of their sweet deception.

The sun grew more intense as the afternoon stretched on, and they felt sleepy, hot, and impatient with nothing much to do until the movie started but peer into their compacts, rubbing layers of mascara, rouge, and lipstick into their faces, failing to make themselves look older—only garish and possibly deranged.

Two boys with brown skin and slick Elvis pompadours circled the block for a second time in an old black Cadillac with white leather interior.

"The one on the right is a dead ringer for Alejandro Mendoza," Ryan said, remembering the Colombian boy the girls had fallen in love with in seventh grade. They would learn the boys in the Caddie were Filipino. Lia was surprised to see two Filipino rockabillies—possibly a somewhat dim perception as she was a black punk, after all. But there were no Filipinos at Coronado High, so what did she know? She only knew of one Mexican boy named Jamie, a green-eyed and blond-haired type, with wealthy parents from Mexico City who lived in a plush condominium down by the beach.

When the boys circled round the third time, pulling up to the bus stop with slow deliberation to the annoyance of honking cards behind them, Ryan gave Lia a look, mischievous and daring, and Lia knew exactly what she thought. Lia gazed at her, wide-eyed with amazement and a sort of grudging admiration.

"But we don't even know them!" Lia whispered sharply. "Plus, how do you even know they're slowing down for us?"

"Oh, I know." Ryan smiled. It was amazing the confidence she assumed around a certain kind of boy, which otherwise eluded her. "Relax. They're just kids like us, not some creepy old men! Besides, we still have, like, six more hours to kill!" Ryan whispered with high-pitched excitement. She yanked Lia up by the arm until she stood, then let go, the two of them sauntering casually toward the car. At least Lia knew that much, to play it cool, to let those boys know they were lucky to even be given the time of day—even though she still felt unsure of herself, a twinge of uneasiness rippling inside.

As they approached the Caddie, the passenger-side door swung open like a treasure chest, and the boy who appeared to be the elder of the two—a young man with the refined and delicate movements of a waiter in a fine dining establishment, wickedly handsome in jeans and an untucked collared shirt—had taken each girl by the hand, helping her into the old car.

The boys were Maximilian and his young brother Jody, a sophomore and senior (a senior!) from Clairemont Mesa. It was Jody, the younger brother, who drove, on *"not even as much as a permit,"* they boasted. Maximilian sat in the passenger's seat, his back against the door, speaking to the girls in profile, frequently showing short white teeth in an easy smile. Their tall, silky black pompadours glistened in the sunlight and made them larger than life.

"We gotta get back home before eight. This is our Uncle Eddie's car. Man, if he caught us taking it out..." Maximilian ran his index finger along his throat to indicate a cutting knife.

"So what grade you girls in?" Jody broke the ice.

"Ninth," the girls whispered in unison.

"What do you do for fun?" Maximilian asked.

"We like X!" Lia chirped, relieved to come up with a tidy answer that was easy for her to share—a short quip with no risk of stuttering or tripping over words.

"Yeah, we're here to see *The Decline of Western Civilization*. It's a documentary with lots of punk bands. X is in it too." Ryan spoke with cool authority.

"Hey, either of you girls sing?" Jody called over his shoulder, eyes steady on the road.

"No." The girls shook their heads. But Lia dreamed it—to be a singer in a band. If there was ever a dream to kill her kiddie past of stuffed unicorns and doomed romances framed in pink, candy floss-tinted windows, that was it: to be the lone girl in a band of boys.

"Too bad. We've got a band. We sound pretty good, if I may say, but we've got a few tunes that could use a female touch."

"That's so cool. What instruments do you play, who sings lead?" Ryan was full of questions. Lia side-eyed her with exasperation for disrupting a dream premiering in real time: Lia, dolled up in a vintage red dress, with red lipstick and a white flower pinned in her hair. *She* would've been the one they'd chosen.

"Max sings lead, I play drums." Jody answered Ryan's question as though it were a test. He reached up then, grabbing the rearview mirror, twisting it like a lens to focus on Lia.

"Really, Lia, you sure you don't sing? You not holding out on me, are you? You look like quite the crooner to me." Lia returned Jody's smile but couldn't keep from squirming in her seat.

"I've never really sung before, in front of people, I mean." Instantly, she regretted sounding so stupid. *"In front of people, I mean."* Jeez, what a dolt. It would be hours later, as she lay awake, eyes wide to the darkness of her room, that she'd realize she should have suggested an audition when she could be alone with them, away from Ryan and brave enough to try.

In the car with the boys, they circled around the city for hours, from downtown to Mission Valley, playing music, stopping at a Jack in the Box drive-through (where the girls refused to eat). The breeze from the open windows gave sweet relief from the overbearing sun, their gallant swains still so young themselves, and thus happy to have two girls in their car—for it was that type of car, that type of California afternoon—it needed girls in the back seat like St. Christopher on the dashboard.

The girls chatted about school (both boys had dropped out) and the boys played The Stray Cats and two of their own songs on cassette. The band sounded pretty good. Max sang lead in a high, clear voice, characterized by a sort of innocence, a choirboy chanting around a Maypole.

In the late afternoon, narrow shadows slanting away from the sun like sleepy eyes, Jody pushed the wide, boatlike car into a vacant lot.

"Lia, get up here, it's your turn." He called out over his shoulder. Lia blinked her wide eyes.

"What?"

"Get up here, I said. When else are you gonna get a chance to test-drive a beauty like this?"

"No way! I only drove, like, once, when my dad let me," she cried. "I don't want to scratch it and piss off Uncle Eddie! You can't get killed because of me!"

Jody laughed. "Come on, it's easy. I'll show you."

She hadn't expected it: being in the spotlight, Jody's afternoon crush. He brought the car to a halt and Max jumped out of his seat and opened Lia's door so she could come up front. It wasn't singing, but it was a kind of audition. It all happened so fast she didn't have time to say no, to protest more vigorously. And the next thing she knew, Lia was in front and in the driver's seat. The seat adjusted so her small feet could reach the pedals, Jody leaning over and helping guide the wheel. What exhilaration! The free-fall weightlessness of freedom, like when she was little and used to swing by her legs on the monkey bars then flip over onto her feet in a cherry drop. In that moment of flipping over and seeing the blue sky as it should be seen, from the vantage of an upturned face, with no constraint of gravity or time, Lia had known bliss—perfect freedom. And in the few seconds she allowed herself to be free, to push that car with Jody's guidance, basking in his admiration and attentiveness, she knew it again. It was the innocent *'weee!'* of a child at play, of being lost in a big, roomy, indelible moment—when anything—all things—were possible.

"Stop! I need out! I'm sick!" Ryan shrieked. For a moment, Lia had forgotten she was there. Her sudden protestation made Lia clumsy so that she laid her foot too heavily on the brake, causing them all to lurch forward in their seats. The car doors flew open and they all got out, horrified at the thought of vomit all over the pristine white interior—forgetting there were other types of maladies.

She didn't puke. Without a word, Ryan pushed past them all, her hair lifted by the breeze as she stomped away toward what was left of the sun, shielding her eyes against its lingering intensity. Lia and Jody and

Max stood around in a circle, silent, not quite knowing what to do. Then, as though suddenly awakened, Lia snapped into the moment, remembering then that she was the best friend, the one who knew Ryan, the one most responsible for her and her inexplicable behavior. Foolishly, earnestly, Lia raced up the block, calling after.

"Ryan!" Then pleadingly, "Hey, are you okay? What's wrong?"

But Ryan wouldn't listen, wouldn't stop. Lia shrugged in defeat and shuffled back toward the boys, tears cresting along the rims of her knowing brown eyes. She questioned what she'd done wrong, and immediately there came the recriminations. She should have refused Jody's attentions. She never should have driven the car and wouldn't have if she'd known where it would lead.

The trio took their places back inside the Cadillac, rolling slowly alongside Ryan, each of them calling, coaxing—courting her back in.

"Come on, Ryan, let's go," Max shouted.

"Girl, snap out of it. We don't want to leave you out here all alone," Jody cried, but Ryan wouldn't hear it. She only shook her head determinedly and kept on. Lia had never seen it, had never witnessed her act this way before. Just as quickly as everything had changed, the afternoon taking on one unexpected turn after the next, prompting a series of divergent emotions, it turned again.

"You know, your friend's a jerk. How do put up with a girl like that?" Jody sighed, exasperated. But Lia wouldn't see it. (She could but chose not to.)

"No, something's the matter. She isn't usually like this." Lia felt alternately so embarrassed by Ryan, and yet so loyal. What choice did she have but to cover for her? Soon enough they'd be back on Coronado Island and she had to survive.

"Well, we gotta get back," Max said. The boys had promised to drop them by the theater so they wouldn't have to worry about getting lost. There'd been talk of the girls coming out to see them play a dance the following Friday at Clairemont High, but Ryan murdered it, destroyed all chances for the survival of their budding friendship—or so Lia thought, not realizing that the perimeters that imprisoned her were entirely self-imposed.

"Ryan, Ryan!" Outside the car, alone on the sidewalk, Lia called after her. She'd known so many emotions in a day that wasn't yet over: fear, happiness, anger. Now everything spun out of control.

Finally Ryan stopped and leaned with her arms folded across her chest against a tree, sweat shining on her face. She stared straight ahead with an expression more lost than angry, and for this, Lia was grateful.

"What gives? What's the matter with you? Why'd you just walk off?" Lia demanded. More than anything, Ryan's downcast gaze called her bluff.

Slowly, quietly, she spoke. "I told you, there wasn't enough air in the back of that car. I felt sick, like I couldn't breathe. I had to get out!"

Lia doubted that very highly, but she didn't want to fight, didn't want the day to be a total ruin. They began to walk slowly down the street in a tense silence.

"I don't even know where we are now," Lia lamented. "Jody and Max were going to drop us off at the theater so we wouldn't have to worry about getting lost. Now what are we gonna do?" She struggled to keep her anger at a low boil, still wanting to see the film, still wanting the day to go back to being a riot—and for Ryan to be her old self.

Realizing that the burden was on her, that she had to do something to make amends, Ryan flagged a passing bus, climbed aboard, and asked the driver for directions.

"He said we need to go this way," she pointed, climbing down the bus stairs. "We have to cross the avenue and get the 150."

They rode along on the bus for quite some time in stony silence until Ryan tossed her hair off her shoulder and turned to Lia with a smile.

"I think there's a Bob's by this theater. I have enough money left for us to split something, a burger and fries maybe."

"We can't, we're dieting," Lia said, tired of Ryan changing the plan.

"Forget it," Ryan insisted. Lia could tell she was trying. "We've still got two and a half hours more," she said. "Shine the diet. We'll start fresh tomorrow."

IT WAS ALMOST UNEVENTFUL, HAVING HECTOR TEAR the verboten tickets in half. His demeanor so sleepy and disengaged, Lia felt prompted to whisper, "I'm Lia, Jesse's friend," as if they were meeting at the high point of some covert mission. The boy only blinked at her, pointing a stubby index finger in the direction of their theater.

The lights went down. This was it! The import of the moment gave them a jolt—a shock of much-needed energy after a long day in which emotions had sapped their strength. They sat alert, but the first part of the film, interviews and performances with The Germs and their manager, was distracting and made them impatient. There was Black Flag singing "White Minority," which Lia thought she understood, but still, it wasn't the main event, or what they'd gone to such lengths to come over the bridge for in the first place.

Just when they couldn't bear the waiting another second, X loomed largely above them on the screen. Exene, her hair shaped into a short dark bob, her lips crimson, commandeered the stage. It was all there, in her stance, her non-coquettish divorce from approval, from any need to be blonde and coy and croon frothy pop songs. She simply stood there and sang, or sometimes growled, pushing crazy, overzealous moshers off the stage with two hands, arms bedecked with bangles, black markings on the backs of her hands. She loomed tempestuously, deranged even, and wildly free within herself.

The shows and concertgoers in the film looked wilder than anything they recalled seeing at concerts they'd attended themselves. And they were in awe, in disbelief that they'd ever entered into venues just like the ones shown on screen. And as much as they admired Exene, watching it all unfold bolstered their perception of themselves also, and made them, for the moment, feel fearless—of every place they'd been and wherever it was they were going. It was then, in this moment, as the grainy footage percolated with life and danger, that they really chose her, anointing Exene with iconic status.

Like love itself, no explanation, no list of reasons could do their passion justice. The lens of their admiration focused on Exene, all others ultimately falling from view. For she was a woman who'd made something of herself, had molded herself into who and what she wanted to be, and this ultimately is what the girls aspired to, though none of this was absorbed rationally at first. They only knew they admired her fearlessness, her power, and truth, which they mostly summed up in pedestrian terms.

"Exene is so rad," they mewed.

"Yeah, she's like, super cool," they chirped, bobbing their heads in unison.

Lumbering off the bus at the bus stop on Orange Avenue, the easiness of warm air and moon-night stars atwinkle masked mortalities yet to be named. The girls were quiet, tired after a very long day, yet still not able to let down their guard—never, as long as they were kids would they ever—so that the story about Crazy Margaret and the cat became forefront in their minds again, just in case it came up as they each snuck quietly inside. They came to the corner of D Avenue, where they would go their separate ways, each one scampering alone in the darkness toward home. They hugged and said good night, one going left, the other opposite, but anger still burned in Lia's chest. If she wouldn't have her school dance, her audition with Jody and Max, she'd have her question. (Though in reality, she was questioning the 'why' and 'wherefore' of it. Herself. And so many other things.)

"I still don't get it," she said.

"Get what?" Ryan snapped with unmasked irritation, turning sleepily to face her in the dark.

"I really wanted to see them again, to go hear them play that dance," Lia insisted.

"You should go then," Ryan said flatly, knowing how absurd it was, her saying that. They never went anywhere, either of them, or did anything of any consequence apart. She would have no more gone alone to the moon, and Ryan likewise never would have gone without Lia.

"They were really cool kids, Ryan. I just don't get why you weren't into them more," Lia said. "You could have at least asked me if I was ready to go. You said it yourself. We still had, like, three more hours to kill!"

"I didn't trust them."

Lia frowned. "What? Why? They were nice. They drove us all over." It was dark, so Lia couldn't prove it, but she could perceive Ryan rolling her eyes.

"There're all kinds of gangs in places like Clairemont Mesa," Ryan said, even knowing herself, deep down, that she sounded absurd. "We don't know who they really are, or what they might be into."

Lia should have known she wasn't going to get her to admit the truth. It's not as if she was going to stand there under the streetlamps, well after midnight, and admit she'd been jealous. Lia turned away, defeated, done—wanting nothing but her bed.

"Hey," Ryan called out after her. "We're still going to the beach tomorrow, right?"

Lia paused. One beat. Two. Three.

"Yeah, I guess." She turned slightly with a quiet sigh. "Call me when you get up."

"Chapter 13," or when our erstwhile heroine catches a brief reprieve from self-loathing...

"It doesn't matter that you give me the money if it's late every time, Neil. It, like, totally defeats the entire purpose."

"That's why I could never get along with you, Cindy. You don't understand the basic things," Neil retorted dully.

Ryan babysat for Cindy Holladay. Cindy was a twenty-one-year-old single mom who lived in a tiny one-bedroom apartment two blocks over. Ryan sat at the kitchen table feeding young Craig, while Cindy and Neil, the baby's father, argued back and forth in the next room, strains of Fleetwood Mac murmuring in the background.

Cindy was short, with tanned, muscular legs she liked to display in cut-off denim shorts. She had streaky blond hair—not so much of the glamorous Southern California ilk, but more in the style of a truck stop waitress. She and Neil had separated shortly after Craig was born.

Cindy stood in the middle of the living room drawing on a cigarette while Neil sat on the couch. All Ryan could see from where she sat were legs. Cindy's short tan ones, shifting her weight from side to side, her small browned foot stamping the dirty carpet with impatience; Neil's stretched out in their pale blue denim, one foot crossed comfortably over the other, his dirty feet in flip-flops.

"Do you know how embarrassing it is to have your landlord show up at work asking about the rent?"

Neil chuckled. "You know what this situation needs? Roses! I should have come offering roses. White, long-stemmed, just like you like. It's been a long time, hasn't it, Cin?"

Cindy sighed. "I don't have time for this, Neil. You either need to be consistent with the payments, or we go back to court."

"Have no fear, little darlin'; that won't be necessary." Ryan saw Neil's taut brown arm reach forward, and she heard the slap of a wad of cash hitting the coffee table.

"Fine, terrific." Cindy relaxed. "Let's see if you can get it right again next month. I've gotta get ready for work."

Ryan saw Cindy's tanned legs moving swiftly away to the next room where she would change into her work uniform.

Neil appeared in the kitchen doorway. Ryan was taken aback. What Neil had sounded like, what she had imagined him to be as she watched him cross and uncross his legs from afar, was different from how he appeared—handsome. His imperfect features sculpted in a mask of poetic nuances that rendered him utterly stunning. He was not very tall, but his jet-black hair, wounded black eyes, and full cherry lips cast the matter of height into irrelevance.

"I didn't know anyone else was here. You the babysitter?"

"I'm Ryan."

Cindy reemerged then in a silly little dress that hit mid-thigh and had puffed sleeves and a built-in eyelet apron. With her dirty blond hair and sullen smirk, the overall effect of the getup was to make her a joyless Bavarian barmaid. She dug inside her pocketbook to find her keys.

"Don't stay around here all night, bugging Ryan," she said, considering Neil with a prolonged gaze. In return, Neil flashed a bold, mischievous grin.

"I mean it, Neil."

"Calm down, princess. I just want to take my time and finish this beer, then I'll be on my merry way." Neil's face split into a heartbreaking smile as he leaned forward to give Cindy a quick peck on the cheek before she had a chance to duck. Ryan noticed the blushing smile that lifted Cindy's pouting lips and poked dimples into her flesh like stars before she quickly reset her face into a straight mask of indifference.

After bending to kiss Craig goodbye, Cindy shot Neil a dirty look as though remembering some pact she'd made with herself and slammed the front door behind her.

Ryan came out of the bedroom after bathing Craig and putting him to sleep, surprised Neil was still there.

"You remind me of a young Jayne Mansfield," he said.

"Who?"

"She was an actress from the 1950s. Totally glamorous and beautiful. Anyway, I was thinking you look like her."

Ryan knew she was pretty, and she also knew that the type of prettiness bestowed upon her was sometimes interpreted by men in a prurient way. Hers was a beauty of the clandestine type, best appreciated through peep show windows and glossy magazines stashed beneath bunk beds. Whereas Lia often felt she was standing in Ryan's shadow, Ryan was always grateful to have Lia nearby. Little Lia, who looked like she was still twelve and dusted her body with baby powder each night after her bath, was for Ryan a shield. With Lia, Ryan felt some remnant of the wholesomeness of childhood; applesauce, nursery rhymes, and the Lord's Prayer were still close at hand.

"You know, beauty kind of goes in cycles. It all depends on what the fashion people in Europe and New York think is cool. Like, in the early sixties, it was that skinny chick, Twiggy. See, you've just got a different sort of look, that's all. If you'd been around during the era of Mansfield or Rita Hayworth even, I can guarantee if I'd put you on a bus to Hollywood, you would have been a star, easy."

Neil was uncertain of how else to tip the scales. He wasn't the type to go in for fraud or grand larceny, and yet there was a searing hunger for something to call his own burning him so hot inside. There had to be a way to get back—at Cindy, and at the father who'd left him only to show up drunk to his thirteenth birthday party with a rusted red bicycle he'd probably found on a junk heap.

Neil felt as though he were at the cusp of forty (although he had just turned twenty-one) because the sweeping slope of his life was heading downhill fast. Prophetically, he envisioned the young boy inside himself cruising downhill on that red bike, poised for imminent disaster.

At long last, someone understood Ryan was a star! The stars were in abundance, gleaming inside her crying eyes, and she thought that this was something she might even be willing to pay for—that in exchange for Neil's attention, she'd repay him with every ounce of devotion she had.

With three older sisters, Neil knew girls. He was a regular professor when it came to understanding about their favorite perfume, the books they read three times back-to-back, or the movies they imagined themselves starring in.

Right before Neil crept out of the apartment complex that night like a thief, just missing Cindy by a beat, Ryan grabbed both his arms and pulled him toward her for one last kiss—but Neil made Ryan wait. He held her at an arm's length so as to get a good look at her—some kid who was all pudgy and beautiful and as overlooked as a dirty orphan—and was pretty sure he had her pegged just right.

Even little girls are entitled to their rage...

THE GIRLS CHARGED DOWNSTAIRS, LOUD FOOTFALLS "like a herd of animals!" shouted Mrs. Payne. Their eyes shone bright with the giddy flame of anticipation. For more than a year, they'd spun records on stereos, every groove and skip a poem they knew by heart.

The purchase of every new album by X was marked like a special occasion. Holed up in one another's bedrooms, they pored over the rich liner notes, inspired by clever, sophisticated verses written in Exene's own beautiful scrawl.

That night, for the first time, they would see them! Exene and the others on stage, all of them breathing and exhaling one another's air in the same room!

Ryan wore straight, platinum tresses, green eyes shrouded seductively by long bangs. Lia twisted blue-black cotton candy into a French roll and fixed it with spray. Crimson lips smiled pinup girl smiles, contrasting sharply with white teeth and the blinding starlight of innocence.

"I wonder how many kids from Coronado will come?" Lia queried as the bus lumbered slowly over the bridge.

"There's a homecoming game tonight, which means most of them will stay put, right where they belong." Ryan was certain.

"Who knows how many of them have even heard of X?" Lia reassured herself.

"Megan Hamilton has no time for punk music; she has to worry about getting together, one by one, with the entire football team..." Ryan quipped.

At this they laughed, their chuckles not induced by humor, or even a genuine dislike of Megan Hamilton, or even the belief that any of the things they said were true—only the need to believe that there was no danger of their thing being usurped by anyone. All they needed was for some popular kids to take a shine to X and there they'd be, homeless as refugees, all the fears and hopes fortressed by those splendid, crashing, cruising sounds—laid bare.

a nymph's cloak spun of silk the moon casts the water a deep, gorgeousdark blue

RYAN LOOKED BEAUTIFUL SWIMMING IN THE WATER AT The Cays at night, the moon throwing a cast on the water that made its surface a deep, gorgeous dark blue. She laughed and twirled around in her white T-shirt, which clung to her body like some nymph's cloak spun of silk. Yet Lia had never known her to risk swimming in the deep waters of the bay.

Ryan had been the first to begin wearing makeup, the first to steal a pack of her mother's cigarettes (and two diet pills), but now it was as if she'd changed, swimming far out to sea, past the point where Lia could reach her.

The girls told their parents they were babysitting for Cindy whenever they partied with Neil. They hung out with him steadily for about three weeks before it all collapsed.

The Cays was a development of condominiums right along the water, where residents docked their boats outside their homes. That warm night, the girls shuffled into the house, feeling their way through the unfamiliar surroundings. The house smelled of new everything: carpeting, paint, varnished floors. It was nothing like Neil's small, dark apartment in Imperial Beach.

Throwing on the lights inside the spacious two-story home, Neil strutted around displaying gleaming new faucets and the glamorous blue lights which haloed the heated pool at night. He offered cold drinks with all the panache of a butler.

"Yep. This beauty's all mine...well, until the job's finished. Soon as we're done drywalling the guest house, the keys go back to my boss," he confessed.

That night, the trio was joined by Neil's friend, a swab named Keith. They sat in the living room, sipping their drinks—beer for everyone except Lia, who preferred 7 Up—while Neil rambled to no one in particular.

"I'm mostly German and French. My last name comes from my dad, but you know, I'm only half...Mexican." Then abruptly, Neil took Ryan by the hand and led her away from the group, leaving Lia alone with his friend: a slight, pale white guy with blond hair and a thin reddish-brown mustache who appeared to be about Neil's age. The sailor did not speak much but smiled faintly at Lia between sips of beer. Each time Lia lifted her eyes to meet his, she quickly lowered them again, wondering what he thought of her, a little brown thing, shyly peering at him like a joey sticking its head out of its mother's pouch.

"What say we check out that pool?" he finally asked.

Lia—artistic, sage, and otherwise mature in her comportment—had not been schooled in the ways of romance. She had kissed a boy once after a seventh-grade dance, and had kissed another at a party when everyone broke off into pairs and he and she were the only two left standing—like P.E. team rejects. She hadn't decided yet if the hasty kiss smacked upon her lips by Ryan's older brother as they passed one another in the dark hallway one night when Lia was sleeping over really counted or not.

Outside, the aqua water in the swimming pool, highlighted in indigo by the illuminating lights, lapped against the concrete—pushed there by the ocean breeze. Beyond the pool and the gate that enclosed the yard, the boats in the marina bobbed along the inlet waters, looking like toys from a distance.

Keith pulled together two white plastic chairs and set them facing the water. Lia ran her hands along her bare arms, trying to rub her chill bumps away.

"I oughta give you my jacket, hold on a sec." The narrow-waisted, light-footed sailor stepped back inside to fetch his jacket.

In the moments of his absence, Lia sighed, ignoring the inner voices that told her she ought to go home. She forced herself to try and relax. Her every move positioned and aligned in accordance with Ryan and Neil; she didn't want to be alone, childishly watching television and eating Cheetos by herself.

The sailor Keith stepped back outside, closing the sliding door behind him, holding the jacket aloft.

He draped the beige windbreaker over Lia's shoulders like a magician's cape and sat beside her as the two of them wrestled with the silence that loomed like a hungry beast.

Timidly at first, and then with increasing firmness, he rubbed Lia's shoulders, attempting to warm her.

"Alright now?"

"Yes," she said in a muffled whisper which fell down into the neck of his jacket, only to disappear wherever muffled whispers go. Over the course of the next fifteen minutes, Lia first let Keith lean against the arm of the chair, positioned in such a way that his arm brushed hers. Then every few minutes or so, he would rub her arms until finally his arm came to rest about her shoulders, shielding her from loneliness, from blond surfers who might have kissed her at parties in the dark folds of night but wouldn't ask her to dance when the school gymnasium was festooned with streamers. He shielded her from her babyish inability to flirt like Ryan, or court danger like her friend Jesse. The sailor Keith created a buffer between her and the sharp edges of reality in much the same way her poems and drawings did.

Beneath the dark, moody sky, in a place where neither he nor she belonged, Lia drew closer to Keith—a stranger, a man from Indiana whom she did not know, a man who sailed endless oceans and had learned to weep silently and without shaking his shoulders in his bunk there on that immense ship with all the other sailors.

Lia learned that Keith had not been raised in a nice suburban home like she had, but had been poor as a child, ashamed that his mother did her washing at the laundromat whereas all the other kids got their jeans and socks washed at home. Yet Lia was a little black girl, so her blackness cancelled out, or was at least equal to, his poverty, and still he had a poor look about him—the evidence was all there: his apologetic gait and awkward mannerisms, his timid grasp of a beer can, his inability to be loud and cocky like businessmen at happy hour or a dozen frat boys slurping beer from a keg. Young Lia, against her best judgment, against the combustible fury of her parents which went everywhere with her like a packet of instant soup, ready to simmer and boil vigorously at any moment (if they ever saw her, if they ever found out!), leaned her head against Keith's narrow, bony chest and let him hold and kiss her. The down of his boyish mustache was surprisingly soft and not scratchy like when her father kissed her cheek at bedtime. Lia got used to him, except for the smell of him and his gray T-shirt which carried the odor of cheap detergent and the muted funk of tobacco.

At first, she had been afraid to kiss him, certain it would be unpleasant, but his taste was mostly predictable, layered in subtle degrees of toothpaste, beer, smoke, and something else—the immediacy of his kindness perhaps, which was surprisingly sweet.

Every now and then, the stranger Keith would whisper, "You're a real nice young lady," and she liked and was grateful for his appreciation of her and also despised it. But mostly she was grateful for being out at The Cays and not in town at the movies on Orange Avenue, for instance, because no one cool would ever be caught dead even giving the time to a swab.

"Damn, this place is really going down. The least they could do is run a mop over the floor every once in a while."

Neil felt it a small yet not insignificant victory that within a mere seven days of their first meeting, he'd managed to coax Ryan out of the comfort of her well-heeled suburb and onto his home turf. At the back of the shabby movie house in Imperial Beach, they sweltered in the heat of the non-air-conditioned theater, a rancid, sour smell wafting beneath their noses.

Neil had taken Ryan to this theater for the precise purpose of rubbing some grit into her face, but the rank odor of vomit was more than he'd bargained for. Ryan only giggled and rested her head against Neil's shoulder. Better to take in the strong, absurdly masculine scent of his aftershave.

Neil was bored by the film *Risky Business*. It seemed that no matter where he turned, he was confronted with the story of some brat. Every good thing life could offer was laid out at their feet, yet they were prepared to squander it, to throw it all away in exchange for the glory of a fleeting taint of sin—for some wrongdoing that might give them an edge but would never leave them wholly blemished, or offset the course of their life of privilege and comfort. The Tom Cruise character was such a twerpy little bastard. Watching him, this Princeton kid, set up a makeshift brothel in his parents' suburban home, seemed to Neil absurd and somehow made him angry and increasingly impatient, so he couldn't keep from tapping his foot against the floor or gnawing at his cuticles as the film played on. He liked the girl character, though, the prostitute played by Rebecca De Mornay, with her slanted eyes and the strong set of her cheekbones. She seemed smart, no nonsense—the type of girl a guy could depend on.

The plot of the film had gotten to the point where it was obvious where things were headed. The smug, self-satisfied kid would get away with what he was entitled to get away with, and everyone would leave the theater with the ways of the world solidly affirmed: young white guys with money were likely to grow into older white guys with even more money, and hell, at least everybody else could be happy for them—someone's got to set the bar for dreams and the stuff they're made of.

Having things to lose, somewhat paradoxically, gave the character in the film things to fall back on. Having neither, Neil was impatient to bide his time.

"To the moon and back, baby, that's how far my love goes. How crazy I am about you." Shutting out the film entirely, he began to kiss Ryan, on her neck and the side of her face, whispering sweetnesses into her ear in a tenderly malevolent tone. "See baby, you're just the thing I've been waiting for all this time, except I didn't even know it. You're the dream, and the dream come true, all rolled into one."

He'd only known the girl a mere seven days! And this fact alone made him want to stop it, to dam the roaring spate of his muddled passions, anger, ambition, determination and love, all fixed in a singular vial, like a drug he couldn't do without.

Ryan was overwhelmed, made nearly delirious by the pace of their courtship. She loved every word that Neil spoke but was hesitant to let go the hold of the thing, the ties of family and friendship, that shielded her from Neil and his quiet yet insistent design.

With the surging of the thing growing stronger, making him almost feverish with longing, although to have the girl right beside him in the theater or in his arms down by the shoreline at night wasn't enough, Neil pressed on. Ryan, hardly ever shy, considered the trash-strewn floor with downcast eyes, the curve of a small dimple belying the delight she tried so hard to suppress. Neil took the soft flesh of her face into his hands, turning her toward him with just enough pressure to both thrill and frighten her. "Ryan, you gotta understand, what I feel for you is serious. A love like this, you gotta take action before it all falls apart, before other things start to intrude."

"What things? I told you, there's nobody, no other guys at school or anything." Here, Ryan paused, suddenly aware of the weight of the confession she was making, and so early on, too. Just a mere seven days into the thing and already she was telling him, assuring him, *'there's no one else, Neil…just you.'*

They fell into a deep, impassioned kiss, and even still, with the honeyed taste of Ryan's lips on his mouth, Neil stayed on task. The film credits had already begun to roll, and in a couple minutes the lights would be on, and he couldn't say what he needed to say with light shining in his face.

Gently stroking her hair, he continued, "I really want some time alone with you."

"But we are alone." Ryan touched his face, trying to soothe away the anguished look clouding his eyes.

"No, no." Neil shook his head resolutely. "I gotta know that I've got you. That nothing's gonna come along and take you away from me. See, what I would say now is that we ought to just get married, but I keep forgettin' you're still in high school. How long before you can take that test?"

"What test?"

"That test that lets you graduate early."

"You mean the GED?"

"Yeah, the GED."

"I think you've got to be at least a sophomore, maybe a junior before you can take that. I'm only in the first semester of freshman year." Ryan sighed. She was secretly grateful for having a built-in excuse, a reminder for herself as much as Neil that she was still just a kid.

Neil kissed her again, and then with a look of yearning that seemed to cut against him like an injury, he said, "I want us to start making plans, baby. The only way I'll ever get to sleep at night is if I know that you'll agree to come down to Mexico and let me marry you there. We won't tell nobody. We'll keep it secret, until you're a bit older, you know, so your parents don't flip out. Just promise, okay, that you'll never leave."

stigmata

EC: Your voice? Okay, I'll give you that. But how many times can anyone sit still long enough to listen to all that syrup just ooze...

RS: It's about singing. Holding a note? That's what I'm saying.

Ronnie Spector had a whole lot more to say, but the argument was halted abruptly so that a tear beneath her right underarm could be scotch-taped before she fell apart entirely.

they fiddled with the collars of their polo shirts, and bemoaned that the highlights created by the Sun-In they'd streaked into their hair during summer had already begun to fade

EVEN WITHOUT RYAN HAVING VANISHED, LIA HAD difficulty concentrating on math. In the sparsely populated study hall for remedial students, they all struggled with the same basic algebraic formula, rolling around inside their minds densely like jeans tumbling endlessly in a dryer yet refusing to dry.

When Mrs. Brenner, the amiable social studies teacher, swept into the class, the collective relief at a distraction was palpable throughout the room.

"Hi guys, sorry to interrupt. Mr. Sengstack and I would like to call all the freshmen together for a special assembly. Can you all follow me to the cafeteria?"

The small group of students slowly put away their notebooks, pencils, and calculators, a dim murmur of conjecture swelling between them. How had they gotten so lucky? What miracle was springing them from math a mere ten minutes into the period?

The entire freshman class gathered in the cafeteria, the meaty smell of the spaghetti they would eat in an hour hanging heavily in the air. Lia noticed Megan Hamilton and some of the other popular girls sitting on the opposite side of the room—their friendship, the time she'd spent on the fringes of popularity herself, had become a distant memory. She gazed at them, thinking not of them, as they fiddled with the collars of their polo shirts and bemoaned that the highlights created by the Sun-In they'd streaked into their hair during summer had already begun to fade, but of Ryan. She was pretty sure one of the girls in Megan's group had lifted a delicate hand to wave in her direction, but Lia quickly sought the floor with a sweep of her lashes. If she could have made herself invisible, she would have. She was too fearful to make eye contact or engage in conversation with anyone, lest they say the wrong thing, or ask her, *'What happened to your sidekick? Where's Ryan?'*

Mr. Sengstack, the high school principal, called the meeting to order. "I expect everyone to be quiet and attentive as Mrs. Brenner makes her presentation. We've called this emergency meeting to discuss a very important...a sad and disturbing situation."

"Let me guess, Charlie Meade's still a virgin!" a boy seated in the back of the cafeteria cried out, much to the delight of the crowd. Charlie Meade was a big kid who spent much of his time alone and was repeating freshman year. Sengstack gazed over the crowd with a stern expression and held an index finger to his lips.

Mrs. Brenner, who had an easy way with the students, paused, her face growing red before she began to speak. A wave of whispers rippled. Mrs. Brenner spoke rapidly before the kids had a chance to make any more interruptions.

"What I have to say to you all today is not easy." The crowd finally settled. "Late last week, we received the unfortunate news that your classmate Ryan Green has officially been reported to the police as a missing child."

Immediately, a collective gasp rose in the room. Everyone was talking in their little cliques, questioning, speculating, conjecturing, whereas Lia felt stunned, betrayed. It was as though intimate secrets of her life were being made public. Ryan's predicament (which had become her predicament) trotted into center ring for everyone to see. Yet just when Lia thought it was impossible for things to get worse, they did, because she heard someone behind her loudly say, *"Who the fuck is Ryan Green?"* Lia felt it immediately: pressure in her forehead, tears stinging like she'd rubbed her eyes after touching jalapeños, and only the suspense of what Mrs. Brenner might say next was enough to keep her bottom pinned to her chair, to stop her from running out of the cafeteria.

"I've had a talk with Ryan's family, and at this time, they're not able to confirm what has happened to their daughter. Now, I can't go into details, but there are signs of hope. The police are searching, and they do have some leads about what may have happened to Ryan."

Lia became more and more enraged. Mrs. Brenner knew she and Ryan were close; why hadn't she warned her, prepared her somehow for all this?

"While you are undoubtedly saddened and alarmed by this news, there are things you can do to help and ways in which you can protect yourselves from being hurt or abducted."

Lia felt that if her anger swelled any larger, she might scream, or faint from the pressure of trying to hold herself together in silence. Mrs. Brenner had been one of her favorite teachers, but now she hated her. She was making everything sound so generic, as though Ryan was just another face tacked onto some poster crying *'Help, Missing Child!'* and not Ryan, someone wholly unique and important in the world

"Personally, I believe prayer is one of the ways in which we can help Ryan and her family at this time. I'm a member of the Christ Episcopal Church, and this Sunday we'll have a prayer vigil, and we're gonna pray for Ryan's safe return..." Lia couldn't listen anymore. The whole thing made her feel sick, the way Mrs. Brenner kept saying *"Ryan, Ryan,"* using her name so cheaply, not understanding the value—the weight—of the syllables she uttered.

"Some of you may be frightened by this situation. We don't want you to go away from this assembly feeling helpless; we want you to be informed and more aware of your own safety. We've asked an officer from the local police department to stop by and share some basic safety tips."

Lia must have been too blinded by anger and confusion to spot him sooner. There, on a low folding chair positioned off to the side of the room, sat the husky officer who'd stopped by the house that day. Watching the officer rise from the folding chair and lick at his lips as he prepared himself to speak, just as she remembered him doing as he'd readied himself to speak to her, was the final catalyst that expelled her from the room. She no longer cared whether every eye in the cafeteria watched her or not. She stood quickly and lurched madly toward the door, like a person desperate to escape a house being shaken down by fire.

"I couldn't get away..."

RYAN HAD GOTTEN A JOB ONE SUMMER CAT SITTING for Crazy Margaret. Crazy Margaret was an old woman who lived in a cluttered Spanish-style house three blocks away with a bevy of cats. She was known for her thick, raspy voice—enhanced by constant smoking—and her incongruous uniform of turbans, patterned house dresses, and fancy gold or silver heels, as though she were poised at any moment to set sail on a cruise.

Lia and Ryan walked over to the house the day Margaret was due to leave for San Francisco. They had to remember to call her Miss Margaret and not "Crazy Margaret," for "crazy" was an appellation given to her years before by some of the older kids, which she wasn't supposed to know about.

Pushing open the green gate, the girls stepped into Margaret's wild, unkempt garden. Cat eyes sparkled in broad daylight. Calicos, Siamese, and ordinary black, gray, and white cats slinked and slithered, or darted and leapt, from all directions. Margaret must have owned at least twenty of them.

"Miss Margaret?" Ryan's tone was all honey.

"Right this way, babe, come on in. My steamer's just about packed." A husky, singsong voice rang from inside.

An old, slim woman, dressed in her own signature high style: emerald-green turban, short-sleeved black polyester jacket and matching pants, tall silver heels. Her body was very thin, yet steel strong, her face caricatured with wrinkles, the scarlet outline of her mouth running errantly over her lips as though painted by a child.

"This is my friend Lia," Ryan introduced.

"Lia! A lovely name for a lovely girl." Margaret beamed, grasping Lia's hands with hers, which were wrinkled and spotted and warm. She held Lia's gaze a little bit longer than most people would have, and smiled more broadly, like a firecracker exploding, than most people would have smiled, and Lia liked these excesses, these peculiarities about her.

Lia's eyes stayed trained on her. She was fascinated, never having seen anyone like Crazy Margaret before. There was something birdlike, some remnant of elegance about her, despite the heavy stench of cat pee in the air and the evidence of past glories, now faded, that clearly marked her face.

"How 'bout a little fruit salad? Hmm? I'm going to fix you girls a treat." Margaret batted her lashes and smiled her broad, too-long smile.

The girls eyed one another with arch expressions, trying not to giggle. Lia felt ill at the very thought of eating in such an atmosphere, dirty dishes piled in the sink, cats slinking and creeping over every surface, including the kitchen counters and table.

Margaret opened the refrigerator door. All Lia could see were half-opened cans of cat food, a six-pack of beer, and a loaf of white bread.

Margaret hummed quietly as she reached into cupboards almost as bare as the fridge. She fluttered swiftly, just like a little sparrow. With a quick jerk of her arm, she manipulated the can opener, flinging open tins of lychee nuts, mandarin oranges, and pineapple. As Lia wondered what in the world a lychee nut tasted like, Margaret continued to whirl about them, oblivious to the filth of her surroundings. She popped open a bag of marshmallows and tossed two great handfuls into the bowl of fruit. Ryan and Lia eyed each other again, now a little intrigued to know what the concoction would taste like.

"A girl's gotta have a treat every now and then. Besides, it's mostly fruits. It won't hurt your figures."

Margaret set two mismatched bowls heaping with fruit salad down in front of them, each mound topped off with a maraschino cherry. "Damn, I forgot coconut. Ah, well, never mind. Bon appétit!" she cried.

Curiosity got the better of them. The girls dug into the fruit. As she bit into juicy chunks of pineapple and syrupy lychee nuts with their peculiar taste and texture, Lia thought, *this isn't half bad*. Later, the moment would be colored by a sweet serendipity that would make it seem as though Margaret had served ambrosia.

After the girls finished their salad, Margaret pulled each of them by the hand, forcing them to their feet.

"Come on, upsy-daisy. I've got ten minutes before my cab. Let's have a little dance."

The girls mirrored each other with expressions of mock horror. With their carefully painted lips and handmade X T-shirts, they were confident they looked cool, so that should they happen, by whatever unlikely circumstance, to cross paths with D.J. Bonebrake, Exene, or John Doe, they'd be prepared. They couldn't dare be caught dead dancing around with Margaret, even if only behind the tall walls of her dirty, madcap house.

Except Margaret wasn't having any of their reticence. "You lazybones are gonna make me late. Have a little dance with ole Maggie, for goodness' sake. Come on..." she insisted, yanking at their arms. The girls had no choice.

The trio stood in a circle in Margaret's courtyard, holding hands. First slowly, then with increasing velocity, they began to spin, faster, faster, round and around.

Ring around the rosie, pocket full of posies. Faster, faster, we all fall down!

Lia lost herself in the free spark of the moment; something about careering around that way, the three of them ageless and giggling, made her so happy.

From the very start, listening to X was the only thing Lia ever experienced that compared to the feeling of that afternoon at Margaret's, of just spinning and spinning, free in the midst of the filthy kitchen of the woman who'd instantly embraced her. Without a word to anyone, or the pursuit of approval, the girls rode that music—faster, faster—until it stopped.

The Wages of Sin

UNLIKE ANY OTHER BOY THEIR AGE ON WHOM RYAN might have developed a crush, Neil changed everything. He took up space, encroaching on territory that had once solely belonged to Lia. Take, for example, the book for Exene.

One the eve of their second experience seeing X in concert, the girls had decided to make a book of drawings and poems for Exene. They planned to stand at the side of the stage, or at the door in the alley behind the theater at the end of the concert, waiting—begging, if necessary—for some roadie or bouncer to let them see her. Failing to secure an audience, they hoped then that some stranger would faithfully deliver their humble offering to their hero.

Yet Ryan had been lax in her responsibility to the project. The fact that the book for Exene, full of drawings and original poems lauding her talents and the inspiration she gave them, was nowhere near being finished in time for the concert, filled Lia with a quiet, simmering rage, because Lia took these things seriously. Between the two girls, it was Lia who'd read *To Kill a Mockingbird* and *Wuthering Heights* several times over and scribed stories and poems of her own.

The plan, in any case, had been to fill the empty artist's book, expressing to Exene their feelings in the honest, raw, and poetic way she expressed her feelings in the songs she wrote and sang with X.

Lia didn't know what was worse: the fact that Ryan had only completed one poem, or that what she did offer was a nauseating tribute to her relationship with Neil, usurping precious lines from X to allude to their sweaty, obsessive infatuation. *"I am the hungry wolf and run endlessly with my mate..."*

"What's your deal, Ryan? We're running out of time. I can't do the whole book by myself."

"I've run out of ideas already. I'm not like you. Poems don't just come to me, you know."

Lia sighed. She knew Ryan was just making excuses. Flattering her in order to get herself off the hook.

"We have four more days. If we work steadily..."

"I don't think it's gonna happen, Lia. I already promised Neil..."

"That's all you ever say. All you ever do. Neil, Neil, Neil. Just forget it then." Lia slammed down the phone, not knowing how to reverse the current, how to stop everything that mattered from flowing right past.

For three years, music had been their highway. All things new and old for them had been a fresh discovery.

The Clash, Go-Go's, Rolling Stones, Doors, Ronettes, Supremes, English Beat, Ramones, and at the pinnacle of everything, X wore the golden crown.

When once upon a time an impending concert would have been the only event monopolizing their attention for weeks at a time (certainly not history, math, or sports), Ryan—the more precocious of the two—had been distracted by the affections of one Neil Jimenez, the raffish, prematurely weathered young man with whom she claimed to be *in love*.

These people ought to know their place, she thought. Then quickly she shook her head. "Damn me. Where does this come from?" her voice a hoarse whisper.

KAREN GREEN SAT ON THE FLOOR IN RYAN'S ROOM, fingering the book the girls had made for Exene. It was filled with poems, abstract drawings rendered in black and red crayon, headless figures sketched in charcoal, and ironic phrases decrying the perversity of love and the dark abyss of a future they might not live to see.

The words scribed in their journal tended toward the morose and poetic. *'Exene is light and life and beauty and pathos, guarding us at death's door.'* Or flippant and immature: *'Life's gonna suck no matter what you do, so party while you can!'* But all of it was sincerely felt, streaming like fractured light from their bursting, expectant hearts.

From what she was able to glean from the journal, it seemed there was a divide between those kids who understood, who felt in their *very bones* the despair, rage, and beauty Exene sang, and those who did not.

For it appeared she had become their muse, the dark icon the girls identified themselves with more and more before Ryan disappeared.

Karen Green touched the thick pages of her fourteen-year-old daughter's book. Bitter tears dropped from her inconsolable eyes like eager skydivers. She shook her head in disbelief. Before the disappearance she'd seen her daughter every day, and still she had no clue who she really was.

At a time when all she wanted was to scream her own brand of punk, Karen Green did not need to be encumbered by unthinkable thoughts. Yet there they were, shining up at her like Ryan's green eyes in a dream she'd had of her the night before, in one of the fleeting snippets of nighttime when sleep deigned to meet her there in the darkness.

Why Ryan and not Lia? They had been together that night, and frankly, Karen Green did not believe Lia's tale: that she'd worried about getting home on time (though it was still very late, past 1 a.m. when she did arrive, and her parents had been furious and sick with worry); that she'd begged Neil to drive her home, and he'd finally capitulated, blindly navigating the narrow landing strip of highway from Imperial Beach to Coronado to drop her off. Ryan, according to Lia, had been the forward one, swimming in a bra and panties with Neil in the pool that night.

Inside the smallest, most furtive chamber of Karen's heart, where half-written notes of truth lay under lock and key, was the ugly, unvarnished question: why Ryan? Ryan, who had the doting, generous heart to be a good mother, if she did not end up a lawyer, an actress, or a nurse. Why not Lia? Sweet Lia with her dimpled smile and good manners.

It wasn't cruelty that made Karen think this way, but only a matter of truth, the natural grain of things, a design quite beyond her construction, really. Didn't it all boil down to a fact of custom and preparation; weren't black people inured to this type of thing anyway? Didn't they have the built-in mechanisms— wailing and flinging their arms about at church on Sunday, blues music and Lady Day warbling her smack-sweetened melodies—to handle tragedy and pain, so nobly, with such dignity and grace? Karen Green didn't intend to be harmful in thinking these thoughts. She loved Lia. It was just that she was confused and unable to make sense out of any of it.

"I wonder how it is for them," Karen whispered as she and Bruce lay in bed, wide awake at 2 a.m.

"Who?"

"The Paynes. You know, to be on the other side."

"I don't get you."

Karen propped herself up on her elbow, facing her husband in the darkness.

"I'm sure they're sorry and all. But sooner or later, this will fade for them. The truth is they don't have a care in the world. Their kid is home where she belongs, and that's all that matters."

Bruce reached for his wife.

"We don't have time for that. We've got to stay focused, Karen. Ryan will be home where she belongs again. She will." Though his words were optimistic, Bruce was not entirely convincing.

"God damn them," Karen hissed.

"Karen."

"Something about it... Something about them going to sleep peacefully each night just gets me. I just feel like, how dare they? How dare they get off scot-free?"

Karen traced her index finger along one of the pieces of artwork in the journal. It was a piece of newsprint cut into the form of a headless woman. She could tell by the curves in the figure—the breasts, curvaceous hips and rounded thighs—that the figure was meant to be female. Written over the newsprint, along the belly of the cutout, headless woman, were words in red ink:

> Your cold lips bring
> kiss of death, to match a heartless heart,
> but I remain unfazed,
> 'cause triumph takes its time.
> My wounds have stopped their bleeding,
> my tears have all run dry,
> I'll survive your duplicitous affections,
> 'cause true punks never die.

Karen couldn't quite make out the handwriting; it became indiscernible as to whether the words had been written by Ryan or Lia, the two of them blended in an inseparable, two-tone, *Tastee-Freez* swirl. Beneath the cutout newsprint figure was a quote attributed to X. The words infuriated Karen because she did not understand: *'Then I died, a thousand times. Maybe you don't, but I do. I've got a hole in my heart, size of my heart. He hung me with the endless rope.'*

Confused and disgusted, Karen gave up trying to understand. She threw the journal across her daughter's empty, lavender-schemed room, where it hit the wall with a short smack—and shuffled into the kitchen to fix herself a drink.

A Shangri-la of hooded eyes, lips shimmering pale pink gloss

ONE SATURDAY, LONG BEFORE A DIVINING SCEPTER struck their lives, the line at Ryan's had been busy for more than an hour. Lia gave up trying to telephone and walked the four blocks over to her house. She had not anticipated a scene. The Green house, never a standard of immaculate housekeeping, was in complete disarray. Records were scattered across the living room floor: The Clash, Black Flag, Peter Tosh, X, along with empty soda cans and ashtrays full of cigarette butts.

Lia had only smelled marijuana once before: the first and last time she babysat for a very high-strung woman living in a dubious row of flats in the more modest part of town. The woman had openly declared her need to get wasted that night and had begun by locking herself in the bathroom for ten minutes before the arrival of her date, while Lia and the woman's pretty little girl (*"Isn't she lovely? Her dad, the bastard, was a Hawaiian I should have resisted but could not")* were left to get acquainted. The smell that hit Lia's nose as she stepped into the Green home instantly recreated the smell of the marijuana wafting from under the door of the woman's bathroom. For some reason, she recollected then that the woman had been pretty enough to be a model, belonging as she did to that ilk of tall, tan, and blond woman particularly favored in that region. It was precisely this fact, coupled with the evidence that luck had done her a bad turn, that added a sourness to the woman's demeanor in the way she fretted over her appearance (constantly running her fingers through her long hair and peering into a compact, her lips pursed as she fussed with their outline in a shade of pink frost) and cursed the fact that she had a date at all. *"Well, damn it, if he doesn't get over here soon, I'm staying home. I mean, I can hardly be bothered. I might have to just keep you on to watch Sienna while I get stoned enough to forget him entirely."* When a short, fiftyish man with a receding hairline and thick fingers finally arrived, Lia was able to read quite plainly every evidence of the woman's dissatisfaction.

As the scent of burning bushes heralded her arrival, Lia learned that Mr. and Mrs. Green, perpetually stodgy fixtures on the living room couch, had actually gone away on a day trip to Los Angeles.

As soon as Lia walked in, Ryan pulled her into the bathroom.

"I totally hit it off with this guy Seth last night when I was sitting for the Baxters."

"Who is he?"

"Mrs. Baxter's nephew or cousin. Whatever. He's totally cute and his favorite band is Black Flag!"

Lia nodded approvingly.

"Is he new here?"

"No, he doesn't go to Coronado. He lives in Oceanside."

Presently, Ryan scampered away for a session of hair curling and eye shadow application.

When Ryan emerged from her room wearing too much makeup, Lia realized she would require hindsight to make sense of everything, because presently, as Ryan introduced her to Seth, she felt a palpable sense of aversion from the boy, which made her feel he did not like her. Yet *how could he dislike me when he doesn't even know me and is meeting me for the first time?* she thought.

"What's up?" Seth nodded stoically. He was a tall, beefy kid, built perfectly for football. He had large blue eyes and a Robert Mitchum cleft in his chin and would have been almost pretty if he hadn't been so sullen, his mouth twisted into a scowl, his azure eyes shrouded by drowsy lids with dark circles like menacing shadows.

The boy did not step forward in a friendly manner after Ryan made the introductions but stood at a safe distance with his hands jammed inside his pockets and raised his chin to her, as though she represented some rival criminal faction.

Feeling uncertain about what to do next, Lia drifted into the bedroom, where she smoothed her hair, re-touched her lipstick, and generally reaffirmed that she was still cute. She then wandered outside, first standing nervously with her arms folded across her chest, and then assuming a deliberately more casual pose by sitting on the front steps. She hadn't met the other boy who evidently was still in the back room getting high, yet Lia held out hope; perhaps he'd be friendlier.

As she headed out the front door, Lia had peripherally seen Seth grab Ryan by the arm and drag her toward the back of the house.

Five minutes later, Ryan stepped out onto the front porch looking sheepish while Lia eagerly anticipated the next step in the plan.

Ryan stood close to Lia and spoke in a low voice.

"See, we were gonna ride bikes down to the water, but there's only two bikes here."

Lia did not immediately see that she was being sketched out of the plan. She simply paused at this information, wondering what exactly Ryan was trying to say.

Ryan could only think to repeat herself, as though this would help bring more clarity. "I mean, I didn't know you were coming. I'd have told you to ride your bike over. See, there's only two bikes here, and..."

"But didn't you say there was another kid here? Isn't he coming with? I mean, couldn't they just ride each of us on the handlebars?"

Just then, the other boy emerged from the back of the house. He staggered into the living room on two thin legs, wearing nothing but a pair of blue and white Quicksilvers. The boy's rosy, plum-cheeked face was obscured by long bangs that fell like a curtain against his bloodshot eyes.

Ryan introduced him to Lia brusquely, as though she were in a sudden hurry to shoo them both away. His name was Charlie.

"Good to meet you, Lia." Despite his altered state, Charlie was affable, much more so than Seth.

Going back to Lia's question about the bikes, Ryan continued.

"Seth is going to ride me on one bike and Charlie'll take the other...I mean, that's what we'd planned..."

But Charlie changed the plan. "Dude, I'm sooo wasted. I think I'm just gonna stay here and munch on some Pop-Tarts, if you don't mind."

It ended up with Seth riding Ryan on the handlebars of her bike while Lia struggled along on Jeff's bike, whose gears she could not manage to adjust to her liking and which was too big and had a crossbar along the top, which she straddled gingerly.

At the water's edge, the odd water rat scurried from behind the shelter of a rock, and a group of young black and Latino sailors popped open beers and danced shirtless and carefree to the voice of a black singer streaming from a tinny-sounding boombox. Seth scowled in the direction of the sailors, muttering, "I hate disco."

Like so many other times, Lia had come along to witness one of Ryan's escapades. Though she sometimes felt left out, like a spectator at a sporting match, a firsthand viewing always brought more satisfaction than a recounting of the facts later. This time, though, she really wondered why she'd bothered to come along at all, because even Ryan looked bored, barely interested when Seth rested a heavy arm on her shoulder. When Ryan sighed heavily, Lia sensed how anxious she was about the exposure of her Achilles' heel: her false, orange-pink, "flesh tone" makeup moved to soup as it began to melt against her face, her carefully painted Kewpie doll mask collapsing from the blood heat of the unusual ninety-degree day.

"Those huge ships are so ugly-looking." Lia did not know the half of it when it came to the unsightliness of Ronald Reagan's tools of war. She only hoped to reinflate a stagnant conversation that had lapsed into complete silence.

Like a lazy dog tempted onto all fours by the promise of a bone, Lia's voice set Seth in motion. Cutting his eyes against the sunshine, he glared at her from the narrow slits he'd made of them.

"When I was only eleven years old, a nigger in downtown San Diego stabbed me in the gut for nine dollars. Nine fucking dollars! I can't fucking stand blacks."

Only later would Lia recover from being stunned long enough to ask—why? Why was it her fault? Why couldn't he see that she'd had nothing to do with it, this stabbing, this robbery?

But that was later. Then, she only felt the heat burning so hot against her back, the palpable rush of adrenaline as she scampered to beat a hasty retreat, clutching dignity like a fistful of sand. She refused to hear Ryan calling after her, "Lia! Lia, wait!" She only felt the butterfly-wing tickle of Ryan's fingertips against her arm as she tried to grab her sleeve and heard the annoying tone of the telephone line pulsing over and over again from when she'd called earlier, and Ryan's line had droned one long, endless busy signal for what had seemed like hours.

like Ziggy *Stardust*
Lia dreams glittery,
shattering, ice cream *dreams*

DROPPING RYAN OFF IN FRONT OF HER PARENTS' house the night they'd gone to the movies in Imperial Beach, Neil felt charged with a crazy energy, like he could stop the Camaro, get out of the car, and leap right there from the pavement on Fifth Avenue directly to the moon! Over and over again, the memory of the devilish little smile that had spread slowly onto Ryan's face as they shared a plate of nachos at Rancho Pueblo after the film played itself inside his mind.

"It would be sort of amazing, wouldn't it?" she'd whispered, her voice husky with complicity as she licked sour cream off her fingers. Her smile was so sweet, but also sort of wicked and dangerous. He was pretty sure he'd got her to latch on to his scheme, to think it over anyway—and that was a start! Or maybe she'd already made up her mind and just wasn't telling him, playing hard to get like girls do.

The thing about Ryan was, deep down inside, she sort of scared him. He couldn't say for sure, but he thought she might actually go through with it, that she might actually agree to go off to Mexico with him.

He felt so proud as he watched her scamper across the grass and up the steps to the front door. He wanted to rev the engine or spin his tires as he left, to make his mark, to convey a *whoop!* of delight, but he didn't want her parents getting ticked off, not just yet anyway. He deliberately dropped her off thirty minutes past her curfew to help get her parents used to the idea that things would be changing now that he'd come on the scene, but he knew he had to walk a fine line, halting at the cusp of their fury before everything was lost and he never saw her again.

Neil was so consumed by his natural, non-medicated high; he knew he wouldn't be able to sleep that night. He thought of stopping off at a bar before heading home, but drinks would only deaden the sensation that shot through his body every which way: a dozen toy cars racing on a track that ran the length of his veins. Thoughts somersaulted inside his mind like acrobats as he considered one idea, only to discard it swiftly for the next. There was the beach, but instantly, the idea of watching the moonlit sea without her made his heart dip, pulling down a veil of melancholy that threatened to obscure his high.

Swiftly, impulsively, it came to him. He pulled the car over to the side of the road, stopping with an abrupt jerk. He dug into his jeans pocket and pulled out a dime as he approached the pay phone. He hadn't stopped to think about what he was going to say as he rapidly pressed the digits he knew by heart.

"Hullo?"

Suddenly he felt a pang of regret. It was obvious from the growl in her voice that she'd been sleeping. He hadn't meant to wake her.

"Yeah...hello?" Cindy's voice rose toward him, garbled, as though she were trying to speak through water.

"Hey, Cin?" He felt panic-stricken and uncharacteristically befuddled. How was it possible that the mere sound of her groggy voice was nearly enough to unravel him completely? Taking off from Ryan's, screeching to a halt beside the pay phone, he'd felt invincible, the world fitting neatly inside his hip pocket. Now he fumbled, fairly stuttering into the telephone. At once, it no longer seemed prudent, calling Cindy to boast about Ryan. Besides, it was premature. What if things didn't go according to plan? What if Ryan slipped right through his fingers just as everything came together?

"Neil-y, baby? Everything alright?" Cindy slurred. He felt so badly then, and he knew it was too late—his broad, immense happiness shattered, crushed to keen shards like a broken hand mirror. Sleep had tricked Cindy into a time machine. Forgetting her anger, her endless dissatisfaction where he was concerned, Cindy spoke to Neil as though still in the flush of that season when she'd been his very own Veronica Lake.

"You know what? I'm real sorry, Cindy. I thought you would still be up. Just forget about it, okay? We'll have a talk some other time."

"You sure you're alright?"

"Yeah honey, just forget it. Sleep tight now."

Neil jammed his hands deep into the pockets of his jeans after hanging up the phone and only managed to walk about two paces before he buried his face inside his hands ashamedly and began to weep like a child.

"she is running..."

In a fledgling attempt at artistry, Lia began to write a journal about Ryan's disappearance. At first, she penned insipid letters addressed to no one in particular.

I miss Ryan, I worry about her. I hope she's okay.

The creation of these stifled missives, though brief, grew laborious. As she read them over, Lia was forced to confront the flat, inexpressive mythology of her letters and figured that if they were to become more interesting, they should be addressed to someone in particular. *'Dear God'* seemed too formal, distant. Lia wanted to communicate with someone who had a face, and she couldn't put a face on God. EXENE. Why hadn't she thought of it right away? Exene would have been the most obvious and appropriate recipient of her epistles. If anyone in the world could understand Lia's mix of emotions, both sadness and rage, it would be her, she thought.

> *"Dear Exene,*
> *I wish you could help me find Ryan. It would be so rad if we could go out on the road together, with flashlights and a search dogs, looking until we found her."*

For the first five days that Ryan was gone, Lia felt satisfied with her letters, as they were both perfunctory and kind. It was not until she'd suffered through the first week of school without Ryan, with whispers and rumors flying down the halls of Coronado High, that Lia began to write of a desperate necessity, more freely and honestly than ever before.

Lia grew sullen, angry, and more disinterested in her classes than ever.

The second Tuesday after Ryan's disappearance, she marched out of Mrs. Brenner's social studies class without the pretext of raising her hand to ask to go to the bathroom. She then sat on the cool marble floor of the hallway, her back against a locker, resolutely determined to write a new letter to Exene. Never mind that tears filled her eyes, that they interfered with her vision and fell onto the pages of the empty book with the purple cloth cover Ryan had given her, blurring her words.

Mrs. Brenner, who'd never suffered any disrespect or insolence from Lia in her class, came into the hallway after a few minutes to check on her.

"Do you need to talk, sweetie?" Mrs. Brenner bent down in order to look Lia in the eye. Lia simply shook her head, her eyes trained steadily on the ground, her mouth a tight fist.

"You know, dear, you really ought to come back into class, unless you want me to write you a pass for the nurse's office?"

"Okay, I'll go to the nurse."

Lia reentered the classroom, trailing close behind Mrs. Brenner. She could feel the eyes of the other students graze her up and over, just as she heard their whispers rustling from behind like hands balling sheets of paper.

Lia took the nurse's pass and fled with it to the track field. Thankfully, there wasn't a gym class or sports team practicing.

She sat down on one of the steel bleachers and continued where she left off, swiftly scribbling an angry note to Exene.

If dolls within dollhouses reside within mansions
then there are books within books and
grim city sidewalks strewn with magnolias

Unable to sleep, Lia crept downstairs late one night, planning to turn on the TV in stealth, and was surprised to find her father still up working at the dining table.

"Hey, baby." She was happy her dad wasn't angry to see her up so late.

"Can't sleep."

"That's to be expected, I suppose." Her father reached across the table to pull out a chair for her.

"What do you think's gonna happen, Daddy? Do you think Ryan will ever come back?" Lia struggled to hold her voice steady. She was tired of crying.

"I wish I could say, baby, but I can't."

Lia frowned. She was hoping her father would have told her something precise, even if it was a lie, such as, *'It's very likely that Ryan will show up again in about three days.'* But of course, her father couldn't say this. Even knowing it would have been a lie, a tall tale spoken just to make her happy, it would have been comforting. A big fat tear fell across her face quickly, like a mouse darting across the room.

Her father took her hands in his. "I can't say what's gonna happen, baby, but I promise you one thing: we're gonna think positive, and we're gonna pray."

Lia studied her father's face and was surprised and comforted somehow to see tears resting along the rims of his eyes.

"Okay." She could barely speak, the tears burned her eyes and throat so.

Her father gave her a tight hug.

"Go on back to bed now."

As Lia retreated slowly back upstairs, Greg Payne breathed deeply. He scanned the table quickly with weary, tired eyes, hoping he still had another candy bar left, but he'd already eaten them all—so quickly, they hadn't had much of a taste, just the texture of something he could grind his teeth against, the sugar of the chocolate and the salt of the peanuts both.

It was a father's duty to reassure his daughter, yet ever since his wife had told him Ryan was missing, the fact of the missing child had stayed on his mind and disturbed his sleep for days.

Though he might have come to it eventually, it was Ryan who forced Greg to face up to all the truths he'd been avoiding, like, maybe California wasn't the answer. The truth was beginning to seep out through imperceptible cracks, like thin veins hidden behind pretty florals on a ceramic vase. All along, months before the fated day Ryan abruptly stopped coming over to hang out with Lia, Greg Payne had already found himself at the center of more than one fiasco.

When he first moved the family out west, Greg had been a fit, handsome thirty-eight-year old, quite pleased with himself on those prophetically sunny afternoons when he drove a rental car up to LA —"*It's true what they say, Ma,*" *he'd told his mother over the phone. "It's 350 days of sunshine a year."*—with Ray-Bans shielding his eyes from the glare of the perpetual sunshine he loved so much. His boss insisted he rent so as not to put needless mileage on his own car—or so he thought, until at least a good two years had passed and Irving Goldstein finally took him under his wing to explain.

"See, Greg, a Cadillac, brand-new or not, is—excuse my language—a coon-mobile. Nobody else drives a Caddie out here except pimps down by the border and old retirees out in Palm Springs. The only reason the boss is footing your rental bill is because he can't have you pulling up to LA clients in that thing."

Greg, a streetwise, big-city guy, felt foolishly befuddled by the whole thing. Though he thanked Irving for keeping him in the know, Greg's pride instantly deflated. He'd always dreamed of buying a Cadillac, not used, but brand-new, picking out any model he pleased and driving it off the lot the very same day. Six months after he moved his family out west, he'd done just that. A brand-new 1980 Caddie in burgundy, the color of rich, red wine.

At first, Greg's possible incompatibility with California life was pointed to by small, nearly imperceptible strokes, like Irving and the car, and then later by more spectacular failures. Perhaps he simply could not keep pace with the Southern California lifestyle—whatever it was or was not supposed to entail. Perhaps he'd been too ambitious; maybe he should have stuck with the Midwest, a landscape he knew so well. But California had been his choice, and Ryan Green was wholly responsible for forcing him to question just how long he could keep pace on the treadmill of perpetual sunshine and good times that were the supposed envy of the rest of the nation.

Long before the girl disappeared—once there, now gone, an assistant in a magic trick snatched behind a dark curtain—Greg Payne was well aware of the cracks, first unremarkable and later obvious, such as the heavy bags beneath his eyes and the fat lapping over his belt like a muffin top, caused by the sheer terror of some exquisite failure stalking him as close as a shadow.

Had anyone ever asked, it is likely he would not have been able to explain why the whole thing with

Ryan bothered him so much. His own daughter
slept soundly each night right down the hall. It was
upsetting, surely, but why did it weigh so much? From
the moment he realized Ryan was gone, his mind was
set. As soon as they found her, as soon as she returned
from wherever she'd vanished, or some conclusion to
the situation had been drawn in any case (he was loath
to think about skeletal remains, telling bloodstains,
or the yellow windbreaker she'd last been spotted in),
they would leave.

He never could have guessed how much he'd long
for the return of certain daily nuisances.

"Lia! It's Ryan." And then quietly, his hand muffling
the receiver: "You just left her house. What in the world
could you possibly have to say to each other?"

It might be days or years, but he would serve his
penance, turning over to Ryan the key to his freedom,
and to Lia's and Dorothea's as well. He felt a sense of
obligation, though not so much the fatherly kind; Ryan
already had a dad, so fraught with worry and beset by
such a wrenching heartache, his thick mane of dark
hair was visibly grayer at the temples a mere week into
the ordeal.

Greg Payne's sense of duty was specific to Ryan; he
loved her. Not in the perverse sense of a grown man
sick with desire for a child, but as a friend. He loved her
raspy voice, breathless and eager when she telephoned
to talk to Lia, as though anxious to report the news of
the world—her easy way of being, treading effortlessly
through minutes of silence as they sat together in the

living room waiting for Lia to finish dressing and come downstairs.

When it came, Ryan's inquisitiveness wasn't rude or intrusive, but fresh and delightful, like an unexpected rain.

"Mr. Payne, you were born in Memphis, right? Did you hear a lot of blues growing up? My dad plays it sometimes, Robert Johnson and stuff, I don't know if I really get it. But I think of you when he plays it. For some reason, it sort of reminds me of you."

Greg Payne smiled broadly. It had not been Memphis but Biloxi. He'd been born and lived there to age six. How could he begin to explain to the child that it was magnolias blooming in springtime that reminded him of her? Her question about blues was what had triggered the memory—of the magnolias, his grandmother, and Susannah French.

He'd returned to Biloxi one summer after his family had already moved to Detroit. They'd made the trip down to gather his grandmother's things and move her up north. As he helped her pack the contents of her small room inside the home of the woman she cleaned for, Greg felt a sharp pang of something his young vocabulary could not rightly name. He only knew that while his grandmother did not preside over a prosperous home full of antiques and fancy paintings, she was noble and grand, yet her grandeur was hidden behind the folds of her worn, molasses-colored face, in the shadows of a small dark room next to the attic stairs.

As Greg folded the framed photo of Jesus that sat on Grandmother's dresser in tissue paper and buried his nose deep inside the bowl of fresh cut magnolias she always kept beside it, he felt overcome by an acute feeling named dread, sadness, or anger—he couldn't say for sure. For in some premonitory flash of knowledge he was too young to fully comprehend, Greg perceived that life was short. Here, Grandmother had toiled away her days, never knowing a single gilded moment. Here was her immaculate room, fresh with the sweet perfume of magnolias. Here was the soft white pillow where she laid a sagacious head of pretty silver hair each night. Here, dreams more grandiose than the black-and-white uniform of household help, or of a prisoner, were woven nightly. Here lay truth, and Grandmother was so wise and free of bitterness, she'd have you believe her truth was delectably sweet.

Susannah French may have been the niece or granddaughter of the woman his grandmother kept house for. She had been about twelve or thirteen that summer.

"Excuse me, young boy."

He'd laughed. Distinctly, he could remember laughing. Young boy. She was *younger* than he was. "My kite's all in a tangle." She pouted. She didn't have to say more; he knew she was enlisting his help.

"What's your name?"

"My name's Gregory Payne." He summoned all the baritone to be found in a fourteen-year-old's voice. He'd been taught, particularly in certain circumstances, to demand respect. He was a northerner, well educated, a student at St. John's Prep.

He'd had to climb the tree in order to unwind the complex web of Susannah's kite string, crawling out onto the near end of precariously flimsy branches, practically hanging upside down in order to untangle the string without cutting it. Twenty minutes into the exercise, he clambered back down the oak tree gingerly, his face and shirt front covered with sweat, swiftly winding the kite string around his wrist with care so as not to tangle it all over again.

Hot, tired, thirsty enough to drink an entire pitcher of lemonade, Greg felt as triumphant as an Olympian as he proudly handed the girl her kite. She must have been near delirium, because she rushed toward him, gleefully flinging her lean arms about his neck. With velocity, her bony, flat-chested body came crashing into his.

"Thank you!" she whispered, her lips faintly grazing his ear. From his feet to his head, Greg was enveloped by a splendidly cold, snowcapped rage. *Has this idiot never heard of Emmett Till?* he thought. *Good Lord, I'd kill her if I could!* The easy fury of a fourteen-year-old boy overcame him then, and Greg was sure he'd choke her senseless. His arms fell quickly to his sides, his eyes lowered to the ground. He was too afraid to lift his gaze, to look over his shoulder and check if anyone had seen, had witnessed what she'd done. He ran from her fast then, into the thick woods behind the house, as though some dread transgression had occurred.

So many years later, who would have thought that by some strangely circuitous route, Ryan Green would be the one, in hindsight, to help him see the events of that afternoon differently? For there was something in her innocent affability that reminded him of Susannah. Some part of him had always known that the girl had simply meant to be as friendly, as cheerful as Ryan, but the laws of who could embrace whom and under what circumstances did not allow for such freedom, such familiarity then.

Perhaps he'd felt angry and shameful all those years because it had been impossible, unthinkable, for him to return Susannah's embrace, yet she possessed the freedom to embrace him, to call him "young boy" in that precociously commanding tone that must have been a mimicry of her aunt shouting out orders to his grandma. Instead of enjoying the freedom of exploration—the desire to kiss, caress, or embrace that came with the heightened sensations so easily visited upon the corpus of a young boy when she'd come careering toward him—he'd had to stomp it away, suppress the natural feelings she'd stirred inside him as though suppressing the dark-hearted desire of murder. Or maybe he'd only felt frustrated by the invisible yet impenetrable fortress that stood between them—two kids too old now to be playmates and unable to fly the kite together once he'd gone to all the trouble of unraveling it.

In the simple act of stealing grapes out of his fridge, in the music of her irrepressible giggles, in her energetic dancing around the TV room to music, in the basic act of watching Ryan converse and joke and play with Lia in the way that people do, Greg Payne was slowly able to let go the fear and shame of that afternoon in Biloxi.

In any case, it was this, the bitterness of fear and crushing indignities, sweetened by the faint perfume of magnolias, which returned to him every time he heard the girls' muffled voices seeping from under the door of Lia's room.

By some odd stroke of luck, Greg Payne had been removed from juke joints in Biloxi, from the easy glimmer of a switchblade on Saturday night, sugar sandwiches when payday didn't come, and Sunday mornings greeted not by church service, but Johnnie Walker stretched out with water. Never mind now— he was in Coronado, and he was free, free enough to take his family to Disneyland every other weekend if it pleased him.

White kids frolicked in his backyard pool like cherubs in a fountain, and Biloxi might as well have been Timbuktu—until his wife told him about Ryan early Sunday morning, and he stopped in his tracks and felt that same steep chill overcome him, enveloping his body like a blustery winter's draft. And for some reason, all he could think was, *Whatever has happened to that girl, by God, please don't let it be one of us.*

Carmine, and rich as spun gold

"BACK UP OFF ME, CRAZY NIGGER!"

Jeff Green was annoyed that, of all things, a vision of his mother's shocked and angry face loomed, interrupting his moment of triumph as the forbidden word tap danced out his mouth in real syllables.

Drunk and high at a house party in Chula Vista, one of the guys in Jeff's group had gotten into it with a black guy—who knows how the argument got started. Maybe it was over a girl, or perhaps it had been about the virtues of ska versus metal? Who knows? Jeff had rushed into the fight to back up his friend. Only he hadn't thought that it would move beyond words— unspeakable words he knew his parents never would have approved.

Blood: carmine, rich as spun gold, spread out in a decadent puddle on the sidewalk. Before he ran off, the young black kid split Jeff's face with a chop above the eyebrow and spilled his blood all over the ground where it spread out slowly, thick as cream for a cat.

At first, Jeff had been afraid to touch his forehead; better to pretend it didn't smart like it did. Then he felt moisture, and Ricky Miller kept saying, "But don't you think you'd better sit down or something? Man, he swiped you good."

At last, Jeff touched carefully at his brow with delicate, probing fingertips. "Damn! Damn!" A thick smudge of red coated his index finger. The sight of it confirmed what the black kid had done, and it was only then that he felt pain—and fury. And Jeff could not, and would never, forget it, so that he developed a taste for vengeance. A sweet, insatiable taste that could linger on his tongue for days.

Little by little, though it went against the grain of everything Karen Green had taught him, that taste for blood—the blood of another strong, arrogant black kid, just like the one who'd hurt him—became an unquenchable quest, like lust, envy, or some other type of malignance that flourishes each day.

WHEN SHE COULD NO LONGER ENDURE THE FEAR, THE twists and turns born of her creative mind about the dreadful things she'd begun to imagine happening to Ryan in pristine detail, Lia took control of the situation the only way she knew how: by recasting the starring role.

In place of the young, insecure Ryan Green, the central character would be portrayed by Exene Cervenka. In place of Ryan's lost, desperate gaze and need to follow Neil's lead without question would be Exene—strong and defiant. With her hooded eyes, lashes heavy with days-old coats of mascara, she would freeze Neil out of his own dirty apartment with her cold stares. Exene would send Neil out on errands to buy her cigarettes and Joan Crawford Red nail lacquer, which she might drizzle quite deliberately onto his dirty shag rug.

Exene, so deft in her portrayal of a fearless teenager, would not minimize her presence in Neil's home. Instead, she would sprawl out on the ratty sofa, forcing Neil to find a spot on the floor, and scratch poems and drawings onto the face of his coffee table with a small penknife. In time, John Doe and Billy Zoom would break into the apartment late at night, visit Neil with a thorough trouncing, and spirit Exene away, her ratty, black-blond hair lifted by the breeze as she ran to freedom down the back alleyway in her bare feet.

is there no greater shelter than my own shadow? she thought

AFTER SLAMMING DOWN THE TELEPHONE ON CINDY,
Neil had managed to sober himself long enough to
make the drive from Coronado to Imperial Beach in
safety. No sooner had he turned the key in the door
of his small, sparsely furnished studio, than he began
to wail in frustration again, muffling his sobs with the
heel of his hand so that no neighbor would hear him.

Neil was just twenty-one himself yet felt as though
he were swiftly approaching death, in possession of a
rare jewel that fit squarely in the palm of his hand and
desperately fearful of losing what he'd found.

As he lay in bed that night, sleepless, a night terror
of fears lurking underneath and overhead, Neil could
see only one thing: Ryan. His focus trained thus, there
was so much more—above and below and on either
side—that he failed to even glimpse.

Neil had inherited the slick black hair of the father he did not know, and did not think himself handsome, even though his face was written all over with a rare, piercing beauty which eluded him because of his obsessive dissatisfaction with every trait that proclaimed him part-Mexican. He loathed the shape of his nose, and when he'd been younger, about twelve or thirteen, he'd spent hours before the mirror, ruing the fate that could have cast upon him such a nose. The fact that his mother's genes had so easily escaped him seemed cruel when it would have been just as easy for him to have inherited her features.

He was also dissatisfied with his height.

"Mom, was my dad very tall?"

"I wouldn't say so," his mother hummed as she put together the ingredients for a chocolate cake.

"Do you remember exactly how tall he was?"

"Umm, I'd guess about five-seven, five-eight."

"Damn!"

"That's no call for cursing, Neil."

He'd skulk back to his room then, imagining himself as a sort of impeccably smooth James Bond character with a last name like Smith or Johnston or Wagner. If it wasn't one bane, it was another: the curse of the wrong nose, or worse yet, the wrong last name. In grade school, the kids teased him, calling him a "beaner" and deliberately pronouncing his last name "gee-men-ezz" just to thrill at his crowning vexation. They were also inexplicable in their cruelty, sometimes calling out, "Hey! It's Juan Valdez!" for no good reason as he approached them on the playground.

He might have given up on his relationship with Cindy because little Craig had turned out to be a doppelganger for him. Or then again it might have been a whole other reason. He knew it was rather perverse, but all along he'd been looking for someone who'd be just like his mother, who'd love him the same way, who could pass her luminous green eyes to their children, finally washing away the stain of that dark thing that perturbed him and made him so uneasy with himself.

As maturity in weariness—if not in years—loomed, he looked back on those early days with Cindy, shaking his head as though to chase the memory away. She had only been eighteen, Neil seventeen, and a baby certainly had not been part of the plan. But Cindy's love had been enough to guide him through those dark months of fear and anxiety as her belly grew, and Neil increasingly dreaded the day when the heap that stretched her skin so would push its way into the world with a shattering cry.

Finding that pleading prayers uttered at a whisper under the cover of nighttime were not enough to stave off the forces of birth, Neil was fully overwhelmed by the arrival of little Craig—a red-faced, squawking thing with a shock of straight black hair that stood on end.

Kicked out of Cindy's mother's house, Neil and Cindy found refuge with his family. His only delight in those days, when the facts of the things that were happening to them at sonic speed were enough to cause a ripe bitterness to suddenly appear inside his mouth, was the comforting circle of women—Cindy, his mom, and his sisters—who would always love him, no matter what.

When Cindy's dad drove his pickup in from Utah to see his new grandson, Neil got it all wrong. The man's lodging, not at home, but at a Best Western eighteen miles away, should have been a clue. Perhaps he should have known better, but when that broad-shouldered, rough-palmed man shook his hand firmly and looked him straight in the eye, offering, "Congratulations, son," Neil immediately caved on his promise to himself and began to contemplate the idea of trying to win his "father-in-law's" respect after all. Beforehand, he had been satisfied with the idea of simply kicking back in indifference, safe within the golden nexus of Cindy's adoration.

On the day her father was scheduled to drive back to Utah, he and Cindy went out onto the back patio for a talk. Neil stayed behind in the TV room, left with no choice but to watch the baby. He handled the boy delicately—because he figured he was pretty fragile— and at a distance—because he didn't like him much, just like a rotten egg.

All it took was one venomous whisper of truth to sharpen Neil's eye.

"Look what you've made of your life." When Neil thought he heard Cindy's father speak these words more than once, in a terse mantra, he lowered the volume on his baseball game to listen more carefully.

What made it worse, what made the incident stay on his mind, was that he couldn't hear Cindy—only her dad. The large man's voice enveloping his daughter's, easy as the whale had swallowed Jonah. A cup of iced tea crashed to the floor of the patio. Neil muted the television completely and stood in a corner of the window where he could see and not be seen, disobeying Cindy's admonition to "never leave the baby alone on the sofa."

Cindy's father had grabbed her by both arms and was shaking her back and forth, her hair whipping all about, her head bobbing like a doll's. Neil was furious then, his body already twisted toward the door—until he heard him.

"You mean you couldn't manage to stoop any lower? With all the boys that's always coming after you, you went and chose a Mexican? Guess I'll leave you to it then. Just don't ever come near me and mine ever again with that filth you chose to lay down with."

Neil gasped, bewildered. No matter who, no matter what, it always came down to the same thing; it was as if he held no other value, carried no other weight.

Who could say what tricked his mind into thinking it would be any better, any different with Ryan? She had bright, luminous green eyes that looked up at him in adoration—the fleeting triumph of a swiftly aging man.

He had one chance yet to show them: Cindy, her father, people on the street who held their purses close to their sides and eyed him with disdain. A daughter of sunny Coronado—not some run-down Utah trailer park, as Cindy had been—had chosen him, and that must mean something.

Of course, Neil had yet to enter the Green household, and he never would. Thus, the portentousness of his imagination was as much to blame for the entire debacle as anything else. The Greens did not dine on filet mignon presented on a silver service, but often ate macaroni and cheese fixed from a box. Mrs. Green did not trot out to do her grocery shopping in cute little tennis whites that showed tanned legs. Neil knew nothing of the ferocious arguments that caused small tremors to ripple through that house when Bruce took out a second mortgage behind Karen's back. If he'd have let go of Ryan's hand long enough to gather all the facts, Neil might not have ever bothered with Ryan in the first place.

if Dinah Shore was passin' in 1979, what does that mean for me? she screamed

LIA HAD FELT BOTH SEDUCED AND FRIGHTENED BY THE scheme Ryan whispered into the telephone that night.

"Just tell your Mom we're sitting over at Cindy's."

"Well, alright...but what if she calls over there?"

"Does she ever? Look, just think about what fun you'll be missing. Neil has the keys to a condo at The Cays. It has a heated pool and everything." Ryan paused to emit what she thought was a knowing little chuckle (except she was fourteen and naïve and didn't know a thing). "And maybe he'll bring a friend for you."

Lia was shy, reticent; yet she didn't want to be left out. She needed to be there to witness it all. "Okay, I guess I'll go," she said.

"Rad! It wouldn't be the same if you didn't."

There were only two black boys in the Coronado middle and high schools combined: Gabriel Clemons and Brad Paulson. Brad, a tenth grader, dated a cute blond girl named Maggie and, as luck would have it, was the more appealing of the two boys.

Lia sat on top of the closed toilet lid in the bathroom at The Cays, watching as Ryan combed out her hair after having swum in the chill waters of the bay. Lia never would have gotten in that cold, terrifyingly deep water. She shivered still, and felt badly, because she'd forgotten to return the jacket draped about her shoulders to the young sailor before he left.

As Lia observed Ryan, she realized she was discovering things about her friend she never knew, like the time she'd gone downstairs late at night to find her mother singing and dancing her heart out in front of the television as though she imagined herself a famous singer.

Looking at Ryan and Neil, Lia didn't know then that there was a difference between love and infatuation. It would take longer still for her to recognize within herself the smoldering rage that made her want to annihilate Ryan, Neil, the sailor Keith—all of them.

Lia sighed, bored now by Ryan's show that night, and angry with herself for being so easily drafted into the plan. She longed for the warmth and comfort of her bed. She would have preferred anything to this, even the hell of sitting sandwiched between her parents on the sofa, eating a dish of ice cream and watching the movie of the week on TV.

As Lia shivered beneath the borrowed jacket of the sailor Keith, she grew more impatient with Ryan's blithe attitude, stretched out on the sofa for hours, tattooing Neil's initials onto the skin of her arm with a straight pin. Lia usually employed diplomacy when speaking her mind, but diplomacy already having turned itself in for the night, she blurted her feelings without hesitation.

"You're acting like a complete idiot."

"What?"

"I don't get this thing with you and Neil. I mean, he's cute, but still, he isn't into anything...He doesn't even surf or play guitar."

Ryan tossed back her head and laughed.

"If you were more experienced, you'd understand."

"Really? What's to understand?"

"Look, Lia." Now Ryan assumed the tone of an impatient adult schooling a small child. "It probably sucks, not having a boyfriend and all, but don't take it out on me."

"I could even see you getting stuck on someone like David before Neil," Lia insisted.

David was the husband of a woman for whom they sometimes babysat. He was a forty-something-year-old man whose good looks vastly outshone his grim, dowdy wife. David liked to flirt with the girls while sipping a martini, his wife cloistered inside her dressing room, squeezing amethyst rings onto plump fingers, forcing pearl cuffs over thick wrists.

"I mean, Neil's not even a punk or anything. He's just scum from Imperial Beach." Lia's tone heightened as she spoke.

"Yeah, well, we all have preferences. Some people might think the same about you because you're black."

Momentarily muted by shock, Lia gazed at the dark flesh of her arm; familiarity had made her forgetful of their most obvious, yet most inconsequential, difference.

Though she was slow to regain the power of speech, what she lost in hesitation, she made up for by pulling no punches.

"Screw you, Ryan!" she seethed. She hadn't been prepared for Ryan to fight dirty. "I was only trying to help." Lia was all earnestness. "Friends are supposed to tell friends the truth," she explained.

"Exactly," Ryan spit back sarcastically.

Unlike Ryan, Lia still went to bed each night clutching that stuffed unicorn. Determinedly loyal and fixated on her dreams, she was slow to catch on.

"What ever happened to our plan?"

"*Our* plan?" Already, Ryan had begun to disassociate from the childishly unrealistic promises of "our" and "we" and "when we grow up."

"Paris. Remember? Study abroad senior year. We were gonna fall in love with an artist who'd sketch our portraits in charcoal and search the Parisian flea markets for lace dresses. Why can't you just wait, Ryan, for somebody decent?"

"Neil *is* decent. You don't know him like I do."

"But..."

"Look, Lia, just let me dry my hair in peace, okay?"

Lia sighed, feeling defeated. She shrugged her shoulders as she walked toward the door, only to hear it slam behind her. Lia couldn't believe just how poorly Ryan failed to see. Didn't she realize how absurd she was, investing so much in a person who was obviously headed nowhere? Then she'd turned nasty, fighting cheap and unfair simply to save herself from a battle she knew she couldn't win, as if race leveled everything, was the ultimate mark of degeneracy.

Leveraging what power she had, Lia broke up the party. Striding into the living room where Ryan and Neil lay sprawled on the sofa of the furnished condominium watching Neil's tiny black-and-white portable TV, Lia raised her voice to a holler and demanded that Neil drive her home right now. In this way, Lia stayed true to form, rubbing something else in Ryan's face: that she was the more responsible of the two, the goody-goody no longer willing to betray her parents' trust by pretending to be at Cindy's to all hours of the night.

As Neil drove her home, Lia wondered if he'd ever discover the little message Ryan left inside the brand-new, gleaming medicine cabinet in ink pricked from the tip of her finger. *Exene rules forever!*

or... because nobody pays Little Richard any mind when he says, "I am the originator!"

"WE ALL HAVE LESSONS TO LEARN. BUT YOU CAN'T ever, ever let any nigger get outta hand like that again," Reggie said. "You keep a sharpened blade on you at all times."

Jeff felt a strain on his spine from holding his shoulders so erect. It wasn't even a conscious thing, holding himself straight in the hope that no one would notice the way his hand trembled as he tried to look casual, holding a beer and keeping company with men. For the first time in his life, he actually had what he wanted, and having attained this success, he'd do anything to keep it.

Along with his buddies, Ricky and Matt, Jeff hung out in the sultry basement in Escondido that Saturday, talking, drinking, and playing pool, while the older guys, Reggie and Stephen, guided their education.

Jeff Green had reached the pinnacle of something, his young life finally in motion. First in the rec room of a condominium in College Park, and later in the Escondido basement of his mentor Reggie, Jeff found himself at one with others. Gone were the days of isolation, of yearning to be a part of something bigger than himself. He was there amongst them, brothers in arms, no longer vulnerable, but safe and protected.

With hatred came a velocity, the lurching madness of careering on a twisting road in a car with no break. There was no certainty of where things would lead, of what would happen next—only the abiding solace that at any moment, something thrilling might occur. At night, he couldn't sleep for the fever dreams that raced inside his mind, his adolescent ego swelling in anticipation of future spates of heroism.

And it was marvelous—the wild rush of air that lifts a sail and moves a boat, gliding along the ocean so swiftly! The taste was sweet, some ambrosia of victory—the culmination of a tense longing, exploding now in ecstasy, in all the light, sound, and color of a million fireworks bursting in gold, red, and green against the sky.

In a corner of Reggie's basement, locked inside a cabinet Reggie had crafted with his own hands, was an arsenal of tools: guns, rifles, lead pipes, knives, batons. "This isn't just a movement, or some jackass social club. This is a war, and every soldier's gotta have his weapon," Reggie had said. Jeff's hair freshly shorn, his allegiance to the group confirmed, Reggie and Stephen, two respected elders in their army, had flung the doors of the cupboard open before his face, bedazzling him with the jewels of a malevolent cause.

Yet it was at this precise moment in his revelry that Jeff Green always panicked; the old feelings of insecurity, of not belonging, of being unable to measure up, resurfaced. In the alleyway behind the Escondido apartment after a session, Stephen, Reggie, and some of the other guys laughed and ribbed each other and messed around with firecrackers while throwing back a few beers. An Asian kid rode through the alleyway on his bike, and Stephen leaped spontaneously into action, pushing the boy to the ground as he rode past—a grown man as quickly animal and thoughtless as a school-day bully. For days after, Jeff couldn't shake the look of terror on the boy's face as he dusted himself off, picked up his bike, and ran, the cruel laughter of the men trailing him like vicious dogs, the unspoken hurt and pleading *why me?* locked in his eyes.

Would he really crack the skull of some Cambodian with the tip of a bat? Take a knife to the belly of that black kid and gut him like a pig? Jeff Green liked to imagine himself at the center of action, defiant and strong, a supernova of rage—swinging, stomping, crushing just as fiercely as the others—but this was only in thought. In reality, the idea of cutting flesh, of smashing bones, left him feeling weary and tepid, that at the moment he was required to take action his limbs would begin to quiver like jelly, and that in a heap he might collapse, a delicate creature swooning at the sight of blood. Jeff breathed deeply after the incident with the boy in the alley, happy to be on the right side of safety in numbers—or so he told himself.

Lia was about the only black person he knew. Sometimes he thought of her. He'd kissed her once. One night she'd slept over; perhaps it had been Ryan's birthday. In the dimness of the hall light, they'd collided, and in an instant, he'd felt a rush of excitement at the thud of her slight frame crashing into his, the scent of baby powder familiar and sweet. Without thinking, without knowing how she'd react, he grabbed her by her slim arms, and in the near darkness, he'd placed a hasty thud of a kiss (not as softly, nor as skillfully, as he would have liked!) on her mouth. After a stunned pause, they stepped around each other hastily, each one going on their way, neither one speaking a word then, or ever acknowledging what had happened as everyone gathered around the kitchen table to eat pancakes the next morning.

He hated it. How the memory of Lia and that kiss floated up to him uncontrollably at times when it was the last thing in the world he wanted to think of. A feeling, something sad or worried or guilty, always came to him then, and he had to stamp it out and remind himself of the black kid who'd cut him and how he needed to get someone back for the gash above his brow.

Jeff fretted needlessly, wondering—worrying—what would happen if any of them ever found out. He'd kissed a black girl! Late at night, as his mind traversed a freeway of grandiose dreams, Jeff Green struggled to summon an intense, burning hatred for Lia, to loathe her as much as he loathed that black boy—*or was it some other black, gaping hole?*—who'd set everything in motion.

"leaves a trail of blue and black, up to you fighting back..." —X

RYAN ACTED UPON NEIL, NOT WITH THE CHARM OF A four-leaf clover, but as a poultice, drawing out his strength in a metaphorical bloodletting that made him weak and feverish. In his weakened state, Ryan took command of the steering wheel, desperate to bring to life the dream that would mend Neil's tormented heart forever.

Along with the sustenance of his blood, Neil's prematurely geriatric state also fell by the wayside as he drew closer to the father he loved and missed so desperately, he'd housed himself inside a fortress of hatred in order to survive each day.

Abandoning the ploy of Mexico once Ryan was at his side, Neil abruptly decided on a detour toward Texas. Speeding just enough to accelerate their odyssey, but not so much as to get pulled over, Neil had begun to head east through Arizona and New Mexico, his vision crystallizing with every inch of pavement they traversed. He did not need Ryan to be his bride, a reticent virgin in a tacky bridal veil—he needed her to be his coach, guiding him along a magic path that would lead him to a prized reunion with a man he did not know but loved unabatedly.

For years, Neil had known that his father made his home in Galveston, and for years, he'd sneered at Texas, loathing every inch of the state with all the ignorant passion of a Klansman loving to tell anyone in earshot just how much he hates blacks. Yet, little by little, day by day, he tested the waters.

"Hey, you know, maybe it'll look too suspicious, us trying to get into Mexico" or "It's just that I'm worried about you, Ryan. You might drink the water over there and get real sick." Finally, he came out with it: "I think we could stay with my Pop for a while, you know, over in Galveston." He spoke the name of his father's city in a whisper, as though it were a sin.

He leaned against the car door, coiled as best he could (given the limitations of car seating) in a fetal position, and looked over at Ryan—her eyes trained on the road with a robotic focus, her two plump hands clenching the steering wheel—and was immediately chastened by the lesson that would set him back along a course of age-appropriate maturation once and for all.

Did he *really* love her, this pudgy girl with belly fat and Marilyn Monroe's sadness in her eyes?

Here he'd gone, telling this sweet, desperate little girl he loved her, when all at once he swiftly realized that like the trick of some apothecary's potion, she'd grown to adore him unrepentantly, while he could no longer be sure he'd ever really loved her at all.

"Would it be of any use, now," thought Alice,
"to speak to this mouse?
Everything is so out-of-the-way
down here, that I should
think very likely it can talk..."
—Alice's Adventures in Wonderland, Lewis Carroll

IN DREAMS, LIA WOULD SEE HER, RYAN'S FORM obscured by a hazy, pastel light, bent over the bathroom sink in the house at The Cays, shampooing her hair. Some mornings, Lia awoke to hear a treble of Ryan's voice retreating as she gained consciousness, as though in sleep, they had shared secrets. In the hazy light of dawn, Lia sometimes opened her eyes to Ryan's ethereal form resting on a corner of the foot of the bed, clamping down on her eyelashes with that frightening curling apparatus, smearing white-beige powder against her baby-fat face, and outlining her small, round mouth in the scarlet rouge of a harlequin.

For three whole weeks, Lia had steeled herself against the overwhelming need to see the inside of the Green family home—the interior of Ryan's room— with her own eyes. She wanted to search beneath the bed and in the closet to prove for herself that Ryan wasn't there. Guilt at living visibly, where her parents and the rest of the community could see her, made her self-conscious. The silence of the Green family left her with the impression that they blamed her in some way; it was as though they were quietly furious that it had been Ryan and not her.

What were the rules in a situation like this? Why couldn't she call and speak to Mrs. Green? She hadn't discussed her feelings with her parents, or asked their opinion, but something—a quiet foreboding— indicated that it wouldn't be a good idea to call. In the first few days, just like everyone else, she'd been anxious for a glimpse, a murmur of Ryan.

When the shock of Ryan's absence had first become known, Lia had been frantic. How to remember, how to get a hold of some talisman that proved Ryan had been alive? When reality took hold and it became evident that she could neither telephone, nor expect to see Ryan running the halls, late for class on Monday morning, stories of where she and Neil had hung out the night before hot on her tongue, Lia searched her room for trinkets. All she managed to unearth was the plastic pink comb Ryan had used to comb out her hair the night they'd fought at The Cays (how had the comb ended up in her bag?) and a half-used bottle of *Miss Dior* perfume from the previous summer, when Ryan had first begun to abandon her girlhood.

It had taken nearly two weeks for Lia to calm herself enough to realize that something other than Ryan was missing: the journal for Exene. As the location of the misplaced journal dawned on her, so did something else: its weight. Lia now had leverage, an excuse. A legitimate reason to stop by the Greens', to reenter that house, to take in the dense smell of dust and cigarette smoke and search for signs and tiny clues.

As time crept forward with the gait of a dinosaur, and nothing emerged—neither the grim discovery of bodily decay nor the thrill of astonishing resurrection—Lia grew impatient. Besides her general feelings of disquiet about Ryan, other deadlines loomed. X was due to play a concert in San Diego in two weeks, and Lia felt duty bound to go, a representative of a small regiment now boiled down to one.

One Sunday afternoon, the air outside warm and fine, Lia mustered every ounce of courage she had and began to walk in the direction of the Greens'. Such was the power of her creative imagination that, for days beforehand, she'd imagined Ryan, wearing shorts and drinking Tab, kicking open the screen door with her red-painted toes, an easy smile spread across her face.

A small black girl with narrow shoulders who sometimes carried the weight of the world on her back, Lia began a slow death march toward Ryan's house.

She had done her best to hold out, spending two weekends in a row babysitting for cash and going to the movies with her friend Jesse, but it wasn't the same. Jesse wasn't much interested in taking the bus over the bridge and looking for dresses sewn in the 1950s, or listening to X. Jesse usually hung around with a group of kids from the military base. They liked to go down by the water at night with cans of beer pilfered from their parents and dance and fling their hair around to Black Sabbath and AC/DC.

Approaching the Green house like she'd done countless times before suddenly felt strange, almost morbid. Lia would ring the bell and could guarantee that no matter who came to the door, it wouldn't be Ryan. On a warm afternoon like that, the front door at the Greens' house was usually open, and Lia could peer inside and see Mrs. Green doing her nails or working a crossword puzzle in front of the TV. Her heart anchored by loneliness, her hand trembling with trepidation as she rang the bell, Lia stood paralyzed on the front steps of the home of her best friend.

The Greens weren't the family outing type of people. It would have been rare for them all to be out together at once unless it was Mother's Day or someone's birthday. Lia quickly pushed the doorbell, took a deep breath, stood back and waited. Nothing. The front door was open, but there was no sound from within. Once more, she laid a timid finger on the bell and gave a short, firm press. Anxiety got the best of her. She imagined someone—Mr. Green, Jeff—looking at her from the safety of the darkness within, shaking their head, muttering, *'Lia will never be admitted into this house ever again.'*

Just as she began to retreat back down the stairs feeling defeated, she heard footsteps and turned to see Jeff's silhouette showing through the screen.

"Lia?" he called out dully.

Lia felt almost haunted by the way he spoke her name, as though she were an apparition and he was questioning, double-checking to be sure he wasn't just imagining her on his front porch. Jeff and Lia, after having shared a kiss two years before, had since developed a relationship of mutual disregard.

To explain now about the book, to enter Ryan's cold, empty room, hardly seemed worth the trouble. The whole thing would mean engaging Jeff in conversation for much longer than she would have liked and wondering all the while what he was thinking behind his trademark smirk.

"Lia?" Jeff pressed on, calling her name again with a nagging insistence.

She turned slowly and clambered up the steps, taking care to center her thoughts and choose her words as she ascended. On a regular day, talking to Jeff might have been a little awkward. Now, she felt too nervous, too strained under the circumstances for small talk or salutations.

"A book. We were making a book for Exene," she blurted. "It should be there, in her room. Unless...well, if everything is still the same. I did as much work on it as she did...maybe more!" Lia rushed to justify her right to claim the journal. Jeff stared at her quizzically, the delay in his response making her feel embarrassed, so self-conscious that she only wanted to run back down the stairs and disappear.

"Hurry up." Jeff gave a terse whisper, his face dirtied by a scowl.

That was it? She'd been granted admission so easily. Where were Mr. and Mrs. Green? She was almost afraid to enter. What in the world would she say to Ryan's parents if they were home?

Jeff held the screen door open with his thin body and motioned for her to come inside with a tilt of his head, his expression still tense.

Lia ambled inside, the interior darkness contrasting so sharply with the sunshine outside that she could barely see. The house smelled differently. Gone was the heaviness of dust, the stale scent of tobacco. For the first time she could remember, the Green house smelled clean, of pine or mint. This change in the environment made her feel frightened. Had they cleaned in anticipation of Ryan's safe return, or as a sort of purging, to erase the scent, the memory, of the youngest member of the family?

All she had to do was pass through the living room and dining room, make a right down the corridor past the bathroom, and go straight into Ryan's room at the end of the hall. For some reason, she paused reverentially—as though she was about to enter a tomb or some holy place, and it was this pause that sealed her doom.

In her moment of suspended animation, there came a distraction. Two of Jeff's friends trailed into the living room, one of them carrying a bowl of cereal. Before their appearance, she hadn't heard a sound. They must have been hanging around the backyard. She only realized then that Jeff looked different. He was wearing a buzz cut and was, for some unfathomable reason, strutting about without a shirt, his pale, bony chest on full display. Like Jeff, both his friends wore a uniform: heavy combat boots, olive-green army shorts, buzz cuts.

Lia was taken aback by the sight of the three boys trooping into the living room like a trio of soldiers. When Jeff had come to the door, she just assumed he was alone. Now that she was inside, it was evident that Mr. and Mrs. Green weren't at home.

"How about a little chat, Lia?" Jeff spoke in a peculiar tone, which was at once both open and abrasive. All along, she maintained her reverence, her concern, her preoccupation with Ryan. Perhaps the boys were forming a search party of their own and needed her to share key information. She'd help as much as she could, but not if it was anything like her talk with the police officer; she could only live through something like that once. Already she'd made up her mind that, if questioned, she'd never discuss Neil again.

"I guess so." Lia walked slowly to the sofa, sitting uncomfortably on the edge.

"Okay, well, just wait a second, alright?" Jeff's command sounded more like a whine.

The three boys huddled together in a whisper, like amateur performers fixing the final touches of a routine.

Finally the trio spun out of their huddle and formed a straight line. The third boy paused to swallow a bit of milk from his cereal directly from the bowl before setting the dish down on the coffee table.

When the boys stood facing her in a straight line and hoisted their right arms into the air swiftly to form an instantly recognizable Nazi salute, Lia couldn't help but burst out laughing.

It was only when Jeff eyed her with a steely glare that made her feel not frightened, but sad, that she realized they weren't kidding. Resting his stick arms on his narrow waist, Jeff declared, "As a protégé of the honorable Reginald Kime, we are duty bound to inform you that race mixing is a sin."

Lia's mouth fell open. She couldn't help but laugh. It was so absurd. But her nervous laughter faded when she studied their hardened faces. Not here. Not the place which had practically been a second home. Surely, it was just a stupid, mean-spirited joke. Or was it? The boys seemed so determined, so proud of themselves. Jeff continued on with his speech as though he'd been rehearsing it for some time. "In spite of what my misguided, liberal parents might say, the bottom line is, I'm starting a new thing and it's probably best you don't come around here anymore."

Lia was dumbfounded, yet certain that Jeff, a permanent fixture in her life (albeit a shadowy one, always hovering in the background), was suddenly, inexplicably turning on her, as if Ryan's silent disloyalty wasn't bad enough.

"What, you mean you're a friggin skinhead now?" Lia stuttered, still in shock. She had always been welcome in the Green home. She'd lost count of how many times she'd spent the night, or how many times Ryan had slept over at her house.

One of the other boys she did not know, a blond kid who was small-boned, thin, and timid-looking, flopped down on the worn, dark green couch beside her and began to speak like a tutor instructing a child.

"Look, race mixing—it confuses people. It's better for blacks to live in their own neighborhoods. Look at you, you're hanging around here in Coronado with all these pretty blond girls when you'd probably fit in better at another school." As soon as he began to speak, Lia realized she'd been wrong about the small, frightened-looking boy, because he quickly gained full command of a strong, beguiling presence as he spoke. "It's not just white people who benefit from segregation like people think. All that brainwashing crap that got started with civil rights in the '60s…"

Lia pondered these words of wisdom quietly. No matter, she thought, that she'd fit in with the "pretty blond girls" better than Ryan had. She'd been a cheerleader whereas Ryan had not. She belonged in Coronado as much as anyone, yet her resolve to claim her rightful place there was swiftly diminishing.

"Yeah," Jeff jumped in, just as anxious to preach to her as his friend. "White people have been putting up with other groups, like blacks and lazy-ass Mexicans who want to come over here and live for free, for too long. We have to start thinking about ourselves for a change."

The weight of their hateful words settled around the atmosphere heavily, making Lia feel like a marionette with dense, wooden limbs. As the words fell from the mouths of the boys, she tried to lift her weary arms and legs, but shock and fear made it impossible to force them into action.

"Dude, you're being way too chill about this." The voice of the third boy, who had resumed his bowl of cereal, rose tremulously at first, then stabilized as he continued to speak. "This is serious. You can't have niggers showing up at your house, ringing your bell. You've got to put her in her place."

The heat of the word *nigger* hit against Lia's face with all the velocity of a slap, leaving her utterly stunned.

She used her hands to help push herself up off the sofa. The miracle meant to come and redeem Jeff, to turn him back to what he once was—which had mostly been immature and annoying, yet innocuous—was tardy, and Lia couldn't afford to wait it out any longer. She bolted toward the front door, Jeff Green's voice rising to a higher pitch as he struggled to assert himself.

"Look—she's like my sister's best friend. She may be...one of them...a nigger, but she's one I've...we've known a long time, okay? You gotta let me handle this!"

Not satisfied with what little defense she'd received, Lia walked toward the door swiftly. She was careful not to run, not wanting to give the boys the satisfaction of believing they'd frightened her.

If Jeff's new political allegiance was stunning, nothing could have prepared Lia for the shove, hard and swift, which hit her square in the middle of her back, courtesy of the boy (she would later learn that she had not been able to place this boy because he was new to the school, a recent transfer) who had been drinking milk directly from the cereal bowl, and whose upper lip was now distinguished by a short, thick, Hitler milk mustache.

"That's right, get the hell out of here!"

Lia scrambled to lift herself off the floor where she'd fallen from the hard motion of his shove and now ran, bursting back out whence she'd come, through the flimsy screen door and back down Eighth Avenue.

a rock 'n' roll star

PUNK IS ALL ADRENALINE AND ATTITUDE, SHE mused—a steady gaze, a fearless tongue, the thrashing rhythm of it a direct transfusion of cocky energy shot straight to her soul. Hunkered down inside Exene's shadow, Lia would be the first to strike, the first to stomp and wail. At least that's how it always went down...*in daydreams.*

Ryan was everywhere, looming larger in her absence than her actual presence in flesh ever had

"I OUGHT TO CALL THE POLICE," GREG PAYNE DRAWLED into the telephone receiver in his provincial Detroit accent.

But Aunt Ola shook her head and ducked furtively toward the window, snapping shut the blinds like a fugitive, the phone receiver balanced on her shoulder.

"Be cool now, police might end up being the cause— not the solution—of even more troubles."

Lia might not have told her parents about what had happened at the Greens' that afternoon, but by the time she came home, bursting through her own screen door, she was panting and weeping, and her palms, which she'd employed to brace her fall, were scraped and bleeding, and there was no way to conceal the evidence of what had happened from her parents because they were sitting right there in the living room as she rushed inside.

"This is not just boys being boys; this is what they call a hate crime nowadays," Mrs. Payne insisted.

For thirty minutes, the Paynes wrung their hands and stifled their rage, suddenly confronted with suburban assimilation issues neither *Emily Post's Etiquette* nor the latest issue of *San Diego Living* could ever help them resolve. Seeking an end to their confusion, they had called back home to Philadelphia, speaking at length to Dorothea's Aunt Ola, a woman who'd spent her entire adult life working as a maid for a well-heeled white family in the suburbs of the city.

"Well, I know you really want to go over there and slap that little fool yourself, but you can't. Whatever you do, don't go to the police first; use them only as a last resort. Try the mama and daddy; if they have any shame at all, they'll whip that boy's butt when they find out."

Taking Aunt Ola's advice, her mother dialed the Greens as Lia watched anxiously. At once hungry for retribution, Lia also found it strange and terribly upsetting that her family was forced to resume contact with the Greens under such odd, uncomfortable circumstances.

As her mother telephoned, Lia imagined the ringing phone on the other side, possibly received by the Greens like a death toll, or the false promise of good news about Ryan.

As she stood and listened to her mother speak, not knowing who had picked up the phone at the Greens', Lia could tell it was awkward—strange for both parties.

"Hello? Yes, how are you? Dorothea Payne here."

There was a pause, silence from her mother's side. Though her hands still hurt from when she'd fallen, Lia remained anxious about the intrusion of her mother's phone call upon the household.

"Umm, huh." Then shaking her head with concern, she said, "I can just imagine. How awful for you. I'm so sorry."

While she wanted to be sure Jeff Green got his comeuppance, Lia didn't want to visit any more grief on his family. Lia and her parents had already discussed all this before the call.

"Baby, we can't just let this go. We've got to handle this now. Ryan is a separate issue. There's just no telling about that."

Then Lia's mother paused, desperate, it seemed, to steady her quavering voice. "Ryan is in God's hands. But we've got to deal with this now; we can't wait on her and pretend nothing's happened. I'm sorry, baby, but there's just no telling about Ryan…"

Lia's mother had embraced her then. A little girl in need of her parents' defense was completely opposite to where Lia was supposed to be heading. She wanted her old life back, the fun and concerts. She wanted Ryan to return, and for things to be the way they had been before she'd ever met Neil. Yet, in some strange way, Ryan was everywhere, looming larger in her absence than her actual presence in flesh ever had.

"I'm glad we had the chance to catch up, Karen, and you know you are in our prayers, but I have another matter to discuss with you. I know things are rough, but there's something we have to address now, I'm afraid. Lia was over to the house this afternoon and..."

At last, the identity of the other speaker was revealed: it was Mrs. Green. Though she didn't want Ryan's mom to be terribly upset, Lia was secretly grateful for the opportunity to twist a little knife into her side. Out of everyone in the Green family, Lia felt most betrayed by Mrs. Green. She exacted the unspoken mandate which suggested Lia shouldn't call   and clearly, stopping by the house had been a mistake. Though she was sorry for the Greens and what they must be feeling, Lia also felt satisfied that they might feel even a tiny drop of the pain she'd experienced that afternoon.

Lia didn't know whether her instinct to cover her ears with her palms and shut her eyes tight as her mother spoke, as though she were watching a horror film, was because she was embarrassed for Mrs. Green to have to listen to what her mother was about to say, or if she herself was too ashamed to relive the details of what the boys had done.

According to Dorothea, Karen Green was in tears over the phone as she recounted the events of the previous afternoon. (The Paynes had opted to sleep on the situation, offering their rage the opportunity to settle before calling the Greens, as it was important that as first-generation, middle-class black suburbanites, they appear staunch and vigilant in defense of their daughter, but not crazy, emotionally high-strung, or, on the contrary, too uppity.)

Chapter I

EXENE IS RYAN. HER HAIR PULLED AWAY FROM HER face in a haphazard ponytail. Her eyes puffy and bloodshot from tears. Without a mask of dirty blond hair to hide behind, her face is vulnerable, exposed like a naked bottom. Yet this face is also stern and determined.

Exene holds one of Neil's heavy work boots in each hand, standing over him as he sleeps like an indolent king beneath the tacky gold comforter of a cheap motel bed. His boots like gold, like the key to a jail cell. Without his boots, she believes, he cannot run after her; he cannot stop her as she flees. She gazes at his face, wanting to remember his rough, unshaven mien—a final glance at some macabre scene, never to be viewed again.

She walks on tiptoe headed for the door, the boots providing necessary equilibrium, balancing her on either side. Two paces toward the door and she is home free. But, before emancipation, a small crisis. How will she open it? She can't let go of either boot, because some fresh superstition keeps her from placing them on the ground. She tucks one between her legs, pressing it tight between her thighs. She will use her right hand to unfasten the lock and turn the knob. Her heart leaps and surges, pumping oceans of warm blood into her body. Freedom: the smell of it moving slowly toward her like the new morning aroma of warm bread. Her palm chilled by a handful of cold brass, her movement suddenly stopped by the rough jerk of her ponytail, snapping her head back.

"Get back here."

"Oh!" A cry. A hard gasp of disbelief. He's discovered her trying to flee.

Eyes hard as bullets, she regards him with ferocious, mean determination. Giving a swift jerk of her knee, she strikes him in the groin. He bends at the waist, tucked over, debilitated by pain. With agile fingers, she unfastens the lock. Dropping the heavy boots with a thud in the middle of the hallway, she runs fast—a little bird flown free.

This is Exene, starring in a film reel in Lia's mind as the character Ryan Green, just as Ryan is Exene in front of a bedroom mirror, addressing an audience with a mournful voice and a scowl. Some of the crowd stands still, utterly enthralled by her performance, while others thrash out their anger in a moment so real—until Ryan drops the hairbrush and sinks to the floor, sifting a dirty straight pin from the plush of the carpet; she takes it to the delicate skin of her wrist, scratching childish hieroglyphics into soft flesh.

Sighting: charismatic figure weeping behind cut glass

"I'M GOING TO MARCH JEFF OVER FIRST THING tomorrow and make him apologize to Lia." During her conversation with Dorothea, Karen Green confessed that they'd only made Jeff take down a flag bearing a swastika from his bedroom wall the week before, and that this new bent, this obsession of his, was peculiar for a number of reasons, not the least being that Karen herself had participated in civil rights marches in the '60s when she was a teenager.

"You know, I think this situation..." Here, there was silence. Dorothea Payne knew Karen was fighting tears, her face scrunched into a neat wad of sorrow. Coming up for air, Karen's voice was distorted, as though she were trying to speak while immersed in water.

"His sister, Ryan. We just don't know...And I think that has made him angry...Not that there's any excuse..."

Dorothea replaced the telephone receiver. "Mrs. Green was very unhappy to hear of this. Can't believe that boy would behave this way, especially when his folks are already having a hard time. Anyway, she said she'd stop by with Jeff tomorrow. She wants him to apologize to you."

Lia's shoulders straightened and she hid a faint smile, as though the visit of the Greens somehow signaled Ryan's imminent return. For ten minutes, Lia badgered her mother: What exactly had Mrs. Green said? How many times had she spoken Ryan's name? Did she say anything, Mrs. Green, about having been visited in dreams by Ryan, and if so, did her dreams hold any clues?

Grabbing Lia by the shoulders to stop her fidgeting, Dorothea Payne raised her voice.

"Stop it, Lia, just stop it. I mean, haven't you had enough? You've got to get a hold of yourself. And what is it with you and this Ryan? Don't you have four, five other little white friends just like her?"

Lia instantly froze, her heart just as much as her body. She was ashamed.

"What...what's the difference? Why did we even move here then, if it matters what color my friends are?"

"I'm sorry, babe. That's not what I meant." Dorothea softened.

Dorothea didn't wish any harm or ill will on Ryan, but she wasn't entirely chagrined about her absence either. In the months preceding the girl's disappearance, Lia had hardly been home anymore. She and Ryan were so busy with their own affairs—habits and interests Dorothea had never really questioned until the morning she received the frantic call from Karen. The thrift store clothes, dyed hair, and made-up faces for history class like dames out of a Bogart film—and the music, that horrible, oppressive noise. Fast guitars like a pile of dishes crashing to the ground. To Dorothea, the whole mess epitomized some anthem of Hades. Still, devil or none, she was grateful to God Lia was safe at home.

"The fact is, baby, nobody knows what's become of Ryan, and you've got to stop hoping so much. I just worry you'll end up setting yourself up for a big disappointment."

How to Eat Your Watermelon in White Company (and Enjoy It)
—Melvin Van Peebles

KAREN GREEN DESCENDED UPON THE PAYNE household in a flurry: large blond curls fashioned by hot rollers; what appeared to be a trench coat in midsummer; and breathless apologies about 'the whole mess' as though Jeff had dented Mr. Payne's car with his bike or thrown an egg at their front door on Halloween.

Lia tried not to feel panicked about the distance that had grown between her and Mrs. Green; one day, everything will be normal, just like it was before. But then there was the added fact that Mrs. Green had changed so much, and this somehow made their meeting anticlimactic, for the lady sitting across from her could have been a complete stranger, some woman muttering to her own reflection in the window of a bus.

Mrs. Green carried extra padding around her hips, and her face was mottled and puffy. She had on more makeup than usual, but it was not enough to mask the exhaustion and weariness behind her eyes. When Lia imagined what it must be like, the toll Ryan's absence had taken, she imagined Mrs. Green gaunt and unable to eat. Apparently, food had been a solace, a faithful friend during night's mute hours.

Jeff Green did not appear alongside his mother as promised for the Green family mea culpa. The Paynes stifled sighs and suppressed the urge to tell Karen off as she rambled in an unconvincing defense of her son.

Lia could tell her mother was furious and doing her best to hold her tongue. Yet the Paynes suffered on, allowing Karen to waste their time as she sat, looking weather-beaten and lost in the midst of their long, beige sofa, talking in a circuitous, sometimes slurred speech—*Was she drunk? Had Mrs. Green taken a sip of some strong drink before driving over?*—about her love for Lia, her abhorrence of prejudice of any kind, and how grateful she was, mind you, to the Paynes for not calling the police because it would have simply ended up "blowing things out of proportion." Because these after all were simply *"ugly child's games,"* and she was certain that this was *"just a phase,"* and that Jeff would eventually *"find his way and grow out of this ridiculous thing."*

Finally, Karen Green thrust a pan of brownies at Lia's mother, chuckling and waving stout fingers. "I figure a little sweet treat always helps…" But Dorothea was not satisfied.

"I thought you said you were bringing the boy over," she said.

Lia noticed a look of alarm pass over her father's face—and she felt it too. She recalled the final minutes of their visit with the police officer, how things had gotten uncomfortable between him and her father, and she hoped the atmosphere wouldn't grow thick with tension again this time.

While Lia and Greg Payne felt a measure of pity and worried that Dorothea's tone might remind Mrs. Green of her grief and bring tears, it seemed she awakened another dormant sentiment entirely. Karen eyed Dorothea sharply, her gaze a challenge that seemed to say, *Oh yeah? Bring it on.* "Look, like I said, I'm sorry about all this. But my boy...Things are tough enough. I just can't be too hard on him right now." Karen turned suddenly from sorrowful to enraged, a puppy teething a bone and glad for something to sink her teeth into.

"Well..." Dorothea shook her head. "Facing us here might do him more good than facing the wrong person in a dark alley someday...This new club of his..."

"Dorothea," Greg scolded.

"I don't need this crap." Karen Green propelled her stout body off the couch, but having stood too fast, she momentarily lost balance, her foot slipping out of a mule that looked more like a house slipper. She stumbled sideways then quickly regained solid standing before shuffling toward the door.

Seeing that their efforts to glean any real understanding about her son's actions had failed, the Paynes felt it just as well when Karen Green finally rose to leave—but Lia didn't. She was frustrated by the fact that the big blue elephant in the room, which was

Ryan, had never once been mentioned. And now she really wanted her journal; heaven knows she'd gone to enough trouble to get it back.

"You can't just leave," Lia blurted. Immediately, the adults' shocked eyes penetrated her from all sides. It can be unnerving when a quiet kid finally lifts her voice to speak. "This is all so crazy. I mean, it's hard on us too, you know. Not knowing about Ryan. We feel awful about it too."

Mrs. Green had been headed toward the front door. Now she turned to face Lia. Lia's entire posture was a demand: for acknowledgement, an answer, a fight, anything but for the real trouble to be swept under the rug. If Ryan hadn't been gone, Lia would never have been alone at the house with those boys, never would have needed to fetch the journal in the first place. If his sister was at home, maybe Jeff would've managed to keep his head, never joining up with those vicious skinheads to begin with.

"I'm sorry." Karen's voice was a hard whisper. Instantly, the nooses of tension wound tight around each of the Paynes' necks loosened, rising into the atmosphere like steam from hot water. They had all felt apprehension at the mention of Ryan's name, not knowing if Karen Green would spin around and slap Lia for taking the name of one who had become sainted—beatified—in vain, or if she would collapse onto the floor in a faint from sheer heartbreak. '*I'm sorry*': they hadn't expected her to say that. They were all poised and anxious now.

"Oh, Lia. You just have no idea. I think about it every day. What it must be like for your best friend to disappear like this. Half the time, when I think of Ryan, I don't immediately even think of her and Jeff playing together like they used to. I think of you. Ryan and Lia, like peanut butter and jelly..."

Feeling like she'd been the cause of her current tears, and reassured now that Mrs. Green did not hate her after all, Lia rushed forward to offer her a hug. But the light, perfunctory pat Lia received in return left her feeling immediately in doubt all over again. Perhaps her parents were right. Perhaps she had no choice now but to try to forget Ryan.

Her face twisted in anguish and wet with tears, Mrs. Green turned away toward the door again.

"I really have to go now..."

As Karen Green rested her hand on the doorknob, Lia thought, *Wait, what about the journal?* It hardly seemed appropriate to ask for it now, but Lia felt it was all she had now, the only tangible thing she had left to prove Ryan had lived.

"Just one last thing." Lia's voice sounded on the verge of shattering.

Karen paused, offering the Paynes a sliver of her profile, as though she were too ashamed to face them anymore. Lia felt frightened. From what she could see of Karen's face, she looked even more frustrated and angry than before.

"Remember when you spoke to my mom on the phone? You promised to have it with you...the journal."

"That thing. Of course, yes. I forgot. It's out in the car…" Karen Green's tone had changed. Perhaps the mention of Ryan's name had made her sullen. Her air was curt, matter-of-fact. Lia trailed Karen to her car at a safe distance. Outside, the sun shone as it always did. It didn't matter whether it was a birthday, a wedding, or a funeral; the San Diego sun invariably struck the same deceptively optimistic note.

Mrs. Green unlocked the back door of her black Thunderbird and leaned into the car, pushing around newspapers and empty shopping bags. Finally, she emerged holding the black, leather-bound journal in her hand. Because Lia had not yet grown to her full adult height, and because Mrs. Green was quite short, the two women stood face-to-face now, the sun gleaming fraudulently overhead.

"Here you go." Karen Green quickly dropped the book into Lia's hands as though it were hot off the stove or dirty and contaminated in some way. Tears had dried against Karen's face, leaving in their wake a thin trail of black and green—mascara and eyeliner—from eye to chin.

"Alright, well thanks…for bringing this." Lia caught the book fast.

"It all still seems awfully hard to believe," Karen seethed. It was as though, far from the watchful eyes of Greg and Dorothea, Karen felt free to let go some of the poison that had lately blackened her heart.

Lia was silent for a few moments. She had no idea what Karen was talking about, what new envelope she was tearing open.

"What is?"

"Every day, Lia, I think about how close you've been to us. How we've accepted you like family. Never— *never*—would I have thought that you would have lied, especially not at a time like this." Emotion rose to the surface of Karen's voice once more, and Lia wanted desperately to flee in face of the hard, accusatory words she spoke, from the fresh commencement of tears dropping from her eyes. Stunned by the surprise ambush, Lia struggled to defend herself, only she was ignorant of the crime of which she was being accused.

"What are you talking about?" Lia snapped in self-defense.

"Don't think for a minute that you have me fooled. Don't think for one goddamn minute that I believe your outrageous, disgusting lies about my daughter! Running around that house all night in nothing but underwear while you turned in for the night at, what, 9 p.m., just like a little angel? I've seen you two. I've watched and observed. You're as thick as thieves. Whatever Ryan does, you do. So why don't you tell me, someone—the police, for God's sake—what really happened the last night you saw her?"

Karen was hysterical, and Lia felt dirty and ashamed. It was as though she'd been hit in the face with a draft of ice water and was still recovering from the chill and the shock, so that she began to stutter. "I did! I told the police everything. I didn't...I never lied about Ryan!"

Tears ran down Lia's face, and immediately, her head ached, as though someone had rattled her brain inside her skull. Karen Green retreated from her then, shaking her mass of blond curls to and fro—in disgust or disbelief, Lia couldn't be sure which—as she stepped into her car.

Lia deliberately dropped the book along the grass and ran around the car to the driver's window. Karen Green had leveled the worst accusations of Lia's entire life, and Lia wouldn't stand for it; she wouldn't allow her to drive away thinking she'd lied.

Gripping the glass of Karen's half open window, tears rushed from Lia's eyes as she cried. "I didn't lie. It doesn't matter what she was doing. I didn't lie! None of this is Ryan's fault. It's Neil! It's all his fault!"

Karen Green only continued to shake her head back and forth and weep, as she turned the key in the ignition and revved the engine.

"Step back now, honey, step away from the car." Karen's voice was thick with exhaustion. For a fleeting second, she had addressed her sweetly, sounding like herself again. But it was all in vain. She had gotten Lia all stirred up but was unwilling to hear her, to listen carefully to what she had to say. Karen sped away then, retreating from Lia's life forever, and thinking the worst of her as she went.

Later, Lia's parents spit their fury in curses and rants, enraged that they'd allowed Karen to get away with a soft touch, only for her to betray them when their backs were turned. "It was pitiful," Dorothea told Aunt Ola. "Came up in here with liquor on her breath, and her nightgown trailing out from under her coat. What's say? Oh, yes, ma'am. A trench coat in this warm weather. Lord's mercy." Dorothea then told how she'd set upon Lia like a wild dog when no one was there to defend her or stop Karen from uttering unspeakable words.

As Karen Green sped away, Lia had stooped to pick up the journal from the grass and noticed that she'd reopened the wounds on her hands from falling at the Greens' when she gripped the half-open window of Karen's car, pleading to be believed.

Thin rivulets seeped, blood gathering into shallow pools inside her palms—and Lia realized that she'd been given a role she'd never asked for. Each day, she sacrificed another tiny piece of herself, her trust, and her good name—for Ryan.

ashamedly, like a little child

"HEY LIA, I THINK YOU FORGOT THIS!" A VOICE followed her down the hallway. She'd just escaped Mr. Brown's chemistry with a hall pass for the bathroom and had no intention of attending any other classes that day. She turned slowly, unable to place the voice of one of the girls from her class. It was Megan Hamilton, tracing Lia's path with soft footsteps.

"Is this yours?" Megan waved a sheet of lined notebook paper. Lia thought it arch, to say the least, that Megan had actually left the classroom to simply return a sheet of notepaper. Okay, so anybody might have gone to lengths to escape Mr. Brown's sedative monotone—*but still*.

Lia froze then, realizing with extreme embarrassment that what Megan probably waved in her hand was one of her poems written for Exene. Lia rushed forward, snatching the paper from Megan's hand as though her quick motion could somehow undo the thing that she knew had already happened: Megan's stealthy perusal of the thing with greedy eyes.

Lia could have stood there in the hallway stark naked and not felt more exposed.

"Give me that!" she shrieked.

"Calm down. What did you think I was trying to do?"

By the time Lia recovered the poem, she was breathless and felt a small tremor of fear quake her entire being. She turned away from Megan, her shoulders shrunken in defeat.

"What is it anyway?"

Lia spun around quickly, anger giving her pirouette a certain velocity. Yet her tongue stalled, making explanation impossible. How could she sum up succinctly that the very reason Megan needed to ask was why she didn't get it in the first place?

Lia wanted, in the most tidy manner possible, to inform her that being coach of the cheerleading squad, having a perpetual tan, and being the ninth-grade girl a vast majority of eighth-grade boys most wanted to make out with, did not mean she understood a damn thing or deserved any explanation about Exene.

Megan was silent, her face marked by a look of confusion. Lia sighed.

"It's a poem, Megan." She spoke quietly, slowly unmasking herself.

"I know, but who's Ex-zene?"

"Exene," Lia instructed with lazy exasperation.

She was impatient to be on her way. She was unsure if the school administration hadn't noticed her new rebellion because she went about it so sweetly, or if they were simply allowing her to get away with a little mischief if it would help her deal with the loss (be it temporary or irrevocable) of Ryan. She only knew that if she took a homemade sandwich over to the football field, she could sit at the top of the bleachers, eat lunch, and pen poems undisturbed for at least an hour until the track team began their relay warm-ups, or the football team showed up to commandeer the field.

Lia turned away from Megan then, lurching toward the field, cheese sandwich and notebook in hand, to take up her self-imposed exile.

"I like it," Megan called after her. "I want you to write one for me."

Lia stopped in her tracks, turning slowly to face Megan once more, her mouth open in shock. At last, incredulity loosened her tongue.

"Exene is special, Megan. She's the queen of punk rock. She deserves poems. She's not just some stupid, bossy cheerleader."

Megan rolled her eyes and placed two impeccably French manicured hands on her hips. "If I remember correctly, Lia, I was the first one to make friends with you when you moved here. I invited you to my eleventh birthday even though we barely knew each other. So, do you really need to be such a bitch?"

Megan had been friendly when she'd first moved to Coronado. As they made the leap from middle schoolers to high school freshmen, they'd simply grown apart without rancor or bitterness—Megan becoming preoccupied with the shopping, preening, and socializing of local fame, while Lia foraged books, record albums, and the dusty corners of San Diego thrift shops for proof of life beyond twelfth grade.

Lia was instantly ashamed. She turned around slowly, allowing her defeated expression to apologize on her behalf.

"Where are you going anyway?" Megan asked. Lia realized then that Megan didn't mean to be intrusive, but each question only made Lia feel more threatened, as though Megan were at her throat with a knife.

"Dunno. Just skipping, that's all."

"Want to share a smoke?" Megan had quickly forgiven her.

Lia panicked then; the weight she carried everywhere, as though Ryan's corpse was draped across her back, was not as well masked as she thought, for there was something in Megan's eyes, similar to the concerned look she got from her parents and teachers, that made her feel uncertain and lost.

"Sure." Lia shrugged.

They ducked into the nearest girls' bathroom. Megan carefully removed a cigarette and a pack of matches from her short, white tennis socks.

"How'd you do that?" Lia marveled.

"Oh, I know all sorts of tricks." Megan smiled.

Megan sat atop the sink while Lia sat cross-legged on the floor.

"Life sucks sometimes, doesn't it?" Lia did not reply because she felt Megan's question was rhetorical, as though she were just thinking aloud.

"I just found out last week that my grandma has cancer." Megan leaned forward, offering Lia her turn at a drag.

Lia looked up at Megan as she inhaled. She had closed her eyes for a moment, as though she were on the deck of a sailboat taking a leisurely tour of the Bay. Lia studied the freckles hidden beneath her tan, realizing that maybe it was the fortress of designer clothes, long weekends in Cabo, her leadership of other girls, and her effortless seduction of boys that had always given Megan's life the illusory façade of easy perfection.

Light rays split dark clouds, and Megan instantly bloomed into something her natural popularity had never allowed Lia to see: an ordinary girl with problems like everyone else. Lia nodded in agreement. For weeks, she'd only been able to see as far as the tip of her nose, and now she realized that she wasn't the only one who was scared.

"You're lucky, though." At this, Lia raised her head in order to see Megan's eyes as she spoke. "At least you've found a way to deal with it. You know...the whole thing with Ryan and all." Megan spoke Ryan's name quietly, carefully. Lia felt foolish. All this time she thought she'd covered herself so well, but apparently her suffering was obvious. Of course, it didn't help that Megan had read her poem. Anger at the memory of this brought Lia to her feet.

"I better take off."

"I meant what I said, you know."

"What?" Lia was still lost in her reflective fog.

"The poem...for my grandma. I'm serious. I mean, it would really mean a lot if you wrote me something I could give to her. I'd do it myself, only I can't write for shit. I got a C– in English last semester." Megan grinned, trying to make a joke of it. But Lia sensed an earnestness, a quiet respect in Megan's tone. She wasn't joking.

"Well, I guess I could give it a try. I never wrote anything for anyone else before."

"Awesome!"

Lia tried not to bristle visibly at the chill of Megan's cold hand squeezing hers. Though Lia had tried to escape, Megan was the first one to leave the bathroom, tossing red-blond hair off freckled shoulders as she sauntered away.

a hellion-voiced angel

WHEN RYAN PULLED UP WITH A SCREECH TO THE small yellow house with the little pots of yellow marigolds yawning up at the blue Texas sky, Neil wondered what it would be like, if his limbs would snap or if his bones would break from the sheer weight, the pressure of being made whole for the first time in his life—because always he'd felt incomplete, like he was half man, half beast. Once he met his dad, he might actually feel human, and the thought of it—like an impoverished child not wanting to get too comfortable with the promise of a full belly—scared him.

With Neil feeling too weak, too faint to do much but stand on two legs, Ryan was the one who rapped at the screen until a short elderly woman pulled open the door.

"Can I help you?" The old woman's face was thin and weather-beaten, but her eyes were laser-keen.

Neil learned then that his father had gone to Houston on business, but here was his grandmother, and later, scurrying from the back of the house, came a gaggle of little children, cousins and half-siblings he hadn't even known existed, grabbing at his hands and twisting themselves between and around his legs, and like side dishes at Thanksgiving, Neil hadn't given the sweet taste of all the little extras a second thought.

not long for this world...

LIA WAS PLEASANTLY BEMUSED BY MEGAN'S appreciation of her work. Megan had forced her to lift her gaze from the top of her Vans and look out at the world. Shutting her bedroom door behind her, Lia kicked off her shoes and pulled the folded poem for Exene out of the back pocket of her jeans, trying to picture how the words had struck Megan as she'd read them:

> Appearing in a halo of pale yellow light,
> Exene, a hellion-voiced angel,
> descended from moonbeams to guide us at night.
> This world of anger and wars—
> so much disquieting noise
> we press our ears against cold windows
> and wait for her cry
> for the glass-shattering voice

of the one who understands why we're
so sad, and lonely, and out of our minds.
We wait in desperation to hear her new songs,
played fast, thrashed out like fire,
and with every razor edge note we dare to believe
we'll live to escape young funeral pyres.

Lia never imagined the poems she'd written expressly for herself would ever be appreciated by anyone else. For three days, homework and favorite television programs were forgotten as she wrote and rewrote, scribbling and erasing words for hours on end to get the poem for Megan's grandma just right.

When she was finally confident that she'd done her very best, emboldened by her new priorities as an artist, Lia did not attend chemistry, but skipped class, waiting for Megan to trail outside with the other kids when the bell rang.

"I've got it," Lia whispered, as though in her backpack, she carried contraband.

"What? Oh, hey Lia!" She cringed. Megan was too loud. If she was going to get her poem, she'd better quiet down and stop drawing attention. She came bounding over, Cecile and Leslie trailing behind.

"What's up, Lia?" and "Hey Lia, how's it going?" The trio of girls happily bobbed their heads at her like cheerful Disneyland characters. Lia stepped back, eyeing Megan sharply.

"Forget it." She spun on her heel, ready to stalk away in anger.

"Ooh, that," Megan remembered.

Lia felt like an idiot. Whereas she'd barely slept for three days, Megan had completely forgotten the work she'd commissioned. Flushed with the heat of embarrassment, Lia quickened her pace. She'd taken a few kind words too seriously.

"Wait up, will you? A lot has happened since Tuesday. I totally forgot." Lia felt Megan's hand tugging at her arm.

"I'm not handing anything over until you shine those two."

"Hey guys, meet me in front of the auditorium in five, okay?" The two girls scampered away.

"It just sort of slipped my mind because we had a quiz today, and then there's the game tonight..." Megan rambled on while Lia reached into her backpack to pull out the special folder she'd made.

With a trembling hand, Lia passed her folder to Megan. At the moment she handed it over, she realized—too late perhaps—that she was also handing over her a tiny piece of her soul.

Megan flung open the folder excitedly as if it contained a love letter from a cute boy. Lia watched as Megan's eyes moved rapidly across the page, taking in her words.

Dear Exene,
Sorry to bother you again. I know I've been writing a lot since Ryan...Anyway, here's one last request—for now. Thanks a million! —Lia

Sing coquette of heaven,
of black diamond sparkle on cloudless sky;
guide us to the firmament,
of sparkling chunk of infinity
where no one ever dies.
Armed with an omnipotent angel's song,
Exene, please keep Grandmother alive.

Megan chuckled. The corners of Lia's mouth instantly tugged themselves into a frown. Megan stared at her, amusement and wonder gleaming from her eyes.

"How weird. I mean, it's totally weird, but it's cool too. It's not exactly what I thought, but I like it." Heedless of the positive words Megan had said, Lia mostly noticed the word *"weird,"* uttered not once, but two times.

"What's so weird about it?" Lia was offended.

Megan smiled a broad, sunny smile. "I didn't mean for you to write Ex-zene about Grandma. I only meant for you to write a poem to Grandma from me, as though I wrote it."

Lia was so embarrassed, she could have died. She offered a shy, apprehensive smile. "Oh."

For nearly three weeks, she'd been so bent, completely obsessed with her petitions to Exene, hoping they would return some promise strong enough to spring Ryan from the clutches of obscurity, that her world had shrunken down to consist of nothing else. She simply assumed Megan wanted her to write to Exene on her grandma's behalf, as though Megan believed as she did, that Exene was in control of some beacon fire that could sear everyone's troubles away. Ironically, Lia really hadn't even wanted to mention Exene in the poem—she'd only done it to be nice—because she was worried Megan would start nosing around, asking too many questions, and the next thing you know, the cheerleading crowd would be giving up their Men At Work and Laura Branigan records to encroach on sacred territory.

That's how it all began: with Megan Hamilton. Megan talked her poem up to everyone all around the school, and word quickly spread. During the third week of Ryan's disappearance, Lia wrote practically nonstop, attending class for the sole purpose of accepting new commissions.

For more than a week, the clamor for a poem to Exene increased daily. Thankfully, Exene's identity (there were only a handful of kids at Coronado who'd even heard of X) didn't seem to matter much. She might have been an archangel or a Salem witch for all anyone seemed to care—everyone only wanted their own personalized sacrament bearing her name.

"Hey Lia," Tyler Wright whispered early one Wednesday during study hall. "I got a surf competition coming up this weekend. You think you can write to that chick—what's her name? Elvira or whatever—for good luck and all? I'd appreciate it."

Lia was overwhelmed by the instant popularity and easy confidences in which she was suddenly embraced the week the poems took off. Such was the demand for her work, she couldn't even use the bathroom in peace.

"Lia, I need to talk to you when you're done." Behind the stall door, Lia grabbed a wad of toilet paper, panicked about who awaited her on the other side. She feared it might be a teacher until she heard the strike of a match and smelled cigarette smoke. She breathed a sigh of relief. Outside the stall, Mary Hitchens, a senior, waited with her arms folded across her chest. Lia wouldn't have believed Mary even knew her name, but she knew Mary—everyone did. She was rumored to be one of the fastest girls in the entire school, a title she'd held since eighth grade.

"Look kid," Mary shrieked. "My period's late three whole weeks! If I ever needed a prayer, a wish, a friggin' miracle—believe me, it's now!"

Through some skewed rumor, Mary had come to believe that the poems cost money—a dollar fifty each, to be exact. She hurriedly shoved fifty cents into Lia's palm.

"That's all I've got right now. I'll get you the buck later, okay? Just write me up something, and quick! I'll never get a Corvette if I'm pregnant!"

"You're getting a Corvette? Like, brand-new?"

"Yeah, on account of the divorce."

"You get a car for your parents' divorce?"

"Not *my* parents, but my dad and his third wife— but she's only five years older, so I actually get along with her better than with my mom...Anyway, Dad promised to get me a car to keep me from slitting my wrists the day he signs the dotted line. Kid, you gotta help me make this problem go away." Mary hurried out of the bathroom, confident Lia would do as instructed.

A mere three days into what would ultimately be her short-lived tenure as poet laureate of Coronado High, Lia's poems exacted a price.

Like any celebrated artist, Lia faced private moments of doubt. She sat on her bed, stumped for words yet anxious to meet a deadline. She owed Steve Harleach a poem first period the following morning. He hoped Exene would be able to assist somehow in getting Cecile Porter to go on a date. "I heard it's easy to get her to go all the way," he'd whispered during English class. Surveying his pimple-covered face, Lia doubted Exene could offer much help, but she pocketed his cash and promised to have his poem by morning anyway.

Besides the happy distraction and flattery she received from her poems, they also caused an increasing sense of fear and anxiety to surge inside of her. While everyone else seemed perfectly contented to clutch some temporary talisman, a fleeting trend of the high school like Nike running shorts or leg warmers cozying the sleek calves of popular girls, Lia was actually aware of another truth: the sole value of the poems lay in their ability to reach Exene through whatever voodoo might become a whisper that could ring inside the ear of one of the elusive fates—and in turn, that whisper's ability to set those frolicsome fates in motion until the forces of their power gathered to bring Ryan home.

No matter what other pleasure or adulation the poems may have garnered, Lia knew that should she succeed in anything short of Ryan's safe return, the cheapening of her art would have been entirely in vain.

a tar baby ain't the half,

X WOULD BE PLAYING IN SAN DIEGO IN THREE DAYS, and the universe offered no indication of what had happened to Ryan. Lia had written poems for the kids at school until calluses marked her fingers, and she was fresh out of ideas.

In the early morning hours before sunlight emerged, young surfers rode their bicycles through the dark and quiet streets of Coronado, their surfboards tucked under their arms. Wide awake a good two hours earlier than usual, Lia faced waves of another kind: fear and uncertainty. The sinking truth was that while everyone else had drunk a fresh batch of a chimera's potion, she was exactly what she knew herself to be: a fraud, her poems as worthless as a bucket full of pennies with holes in them.

For four long weeks, she'd written invocation upon invocation to Exene, pasting them on the walls of her room and in the metal vault of her locker. At night, she rested on bended knee in front of flaming candles to offer her supplications—and nothing. Mary Hitchens happily proclaimed to anyone who'd listen that it was a false alarm; she wasn't pregnant. Megan Hamilton's grandmother was in remission, and for all intents and purposes, Ryan was as good as dead.

"Nothing seems real anymore," Lia muttered to herself as she removed eye makeup she'd failed to take off the previous day so she could reapply it before class.

God had to know that, in reality, her prayers were intended for Him. Exene was just her chosen conduit, the moody icon who would never look down at Lia in judgment, but who beckoned with the siren powers of someone tempestuous yet sympathetic and compassionate.

OR WOULD SHE BE? WHAT WOULD EXENE HAVE REALLY thought of her if they ever stood face-to-face, the black kid who bought concert tickets and albums like all the other kids? (She'd spotted an older black guy, maybe in his twenties, right down by the front of the stage at one of their first concerts and had thought, hooray, I'm not the only one!)

Maybe Exene was just like all the other angels, looking down on her and Ryan from some lofty pedestal, too bored and disinterested to lift a dirty wing to come to their aid. Perhaps Exene wasn't the sort of angel who cared to be bothered with the prayers of young black girls. Maybe what Lia needed to do was get Megan Hamilton to beseech Exene on her behalf.

Ryan was scared, but still, I've got to keep going, she thought.

LIA CRANKED THE VOLUME AND DID AN ERRATIC, JERKY dance around the room, baiting her father's wrath because twice he'd already told her to "quit thumping around up there!" But that didn't stop her; only a cold realization did. Was the "nigger" Jeff Green's friend had hollered at her the same one Exene meant in the song "Los Angeles"? In other words: *her?*

A Supreme Fraud

On the day of the concert, Lia kept a vigil. Ten, eleven, noon...the day dragged on and not a word about Ryan. In her mind, not so far removed yet from a child's realm of fairytale endings all but presented in birthday wrapping and tied in a pretty bow, she'd felt quite certain that Ryan would come home safely in time for the concert as a sign that some celestial creature had heard her prayers.

In the eleventh hour, even Lia felt that things would have been so much easier if she'd vanished instead of Ryan. On the one hand, it would have made a good story. As one of only a tiny handful of black girls (what, were there three, four others in the entire town?), Lia's story would have stood out. Everyone's attention would have been captured by the sweet-faced, dimpled-smiled girl staring out innocently from the newspaper photos. And yet, as time went on, the story would have faded much quicker.

Just as Karen Green silently hypothesized, the community would have mourned Lia's loss with the subtly veiled understanding that, oh well, black people are used to tragedy anyway, what with inner-city tenement fires, sickle cell anemia, and police brutality—there was always something, some perpetually dark curtain poised to fall upon them. The loss of a young white girl created a great deal more pressure for everyone, and Lia felt feeble under its groaning weight. The police, teachers at school, the Green family—all felt time bearing down on them at a great pace, so that Mrs. Green spent her days winding yellow ribbons around trees all across the front lawns and parks of Coronado, uncertain of how else to respond to her sudden place in the public eye as the mother of the missing girl.

By the fourth week of Ryan's disappearance, Mrs. Boyle, Ryan's homeroom teacher, unsure of what else she could possibly do, had held two bake sales and one raffle (first prize a Gillette hair dryer) for what she called the Ryan Green Safe Return Fund. The proceeds were supposedly being contributed to the local police department in order to help in defraying the cost of search efforts. And Lia, as though the invisible eyes of judgment were watching her every move, felt that as Ryan's closest friend, she had to maintain a ceaseless vigil. The truth was, Ryan was on her mind all the time—such that she'd bought not one, but two tickets to see X play that night, with the fatalistic hope that her gesture of confidence would be reciprocated by Ryan's secure and timely homecoming. (Was it possible? Could Ryan really come home by noon or even 3 p.m. and make it to the concert that night?)

All day, Lia jumped as the phone rang, but never once did the party on the other end offer a word about her best friend. As dusk began its descent over the city, Lia's stomach muscles tensed. Anger cut her in fragmented pieces, yet she could easily piece together the shards to form a mirror of her seething rage at having to suffer insults. Like puny Jeff Green and his menacing pro-Nazi B.S. Like why the hell didn't Ryan either come home already or die and get it over with? Like loving X yet fearing she wouldn't have any way to separate the punks from the neo-Nazi skinheads who might show up to the concert. Like knowing if anyone could understand isolation, a loathsome dread of suburban idle, it was she, and yet melanin did her a disservice as far as bearing the appearance of an authentic punk was concerned.

She gamely blackened her eyes and smattered her lips Old Hollywood Red. She realized there was a certain irony in the fact that she'd donned the festive, almost giddy pink dress that Ryan had found for her at the Salvation Army, whereas inside, she scarcely felt festive or celebratory. To make this point clear to anyone adept at observation, Lia topped off the outfit not with the pink satin pumps she'd found for a dollar and which matched the dress perfectly, but with a pair of worn black flats, scuffed at the heel and bearing a small hole at the toe.

As she slid her feet into the shoes, she sang the lyrics to her favorite X song.

"The world's a mess, it's in my kiss." And it was.

once a long-awaited moment arrives ... then what?

"BUT WHO'S GOING TO THE CONCERT WITH YOU?"

"I'll be all alone either way," she muttered to herself.

"What say, baby?"

Hovering far and above her like helium balloons loosened from the grasp of a child, Lia's parents inched each day a bit further into oblivion. Complete freedom and not the direct communication of words was the consolation they offered in the absence of her best friend. How long would they have to indulge her, to grant her such perimeters of freedom? No one knew.

In any case, when Lia told them she was (bravely, fearlessly) taking off for the concert in San Diego, her father only quietly inquired, in a delicate tone, "You meeting friends there, baby?" She would have felt lonely even if she did have someone to go with. But because she didn't, she quickly came up with, "Yeah, Megan Hamilton. We used to do cheerleading together."

Lia boarded the last bus bound for San Diego in order to prove her valiance, the journal she hoped to give Exene tucked under her arm.

Mandatory Curse

AFTER GETTING OFF THE BUS AND WALKING THREE blocks to the concert venue, Lia felt a thrill! A long line of concertgoers had already formed, other kids in their Levis, torn T-shirts, vintage dresses, dyed hair, and devil-may-care posturing. X was playing and it was going to be big!

She shuffled up to the end of the line with the stance of someone who didn't want to be noticed, who only wished to blend in as though she were camouflaged. She clutched the journal tight inside her hand and threw back her shoulders, distinguished from the crowd by the loftiness of her mission, like a clergyman clutching a bible. While holding out hope about Ryan up until the final moment, Lia had worked furiously to complete the book for Exene—the same book Ryan had abandoned and Mrs. Green had nearly cast to the ground.

After waiting in line for more than thirty minutes, once security flung open the doors, Lia allowed the surge of the crowd to carry her into the ballroom as though on a wave. Lia was sad to be alone, and yet thrilled as she waited for Exene to take the stage, like anticipating a queen on her coronation day.

After suffering the unappealing drone of the opening act, X finally took the stage. Excited, hyped with energy, the crowd surged forward as Billy Zoom struck his guitar, the opening notes of "Johnny Hit and Run Paulene" alive and in the air, and the sound was exhilarating. Exene appeared after the song had begun, just in time to lean into the microphone and harmonize sparse phrases with John Doe. She looked even more amazing than Lia had imagined. Her hair had thicker blond streaks in contrast with dark brown than the photo on the last album had shown. Her eyes had been blackened to a narrow defiance. Her mouth was a sneering vermillion pucker. Between verses, Exene boldly turned her back on the audience, epitomizing cool defiance. Lia only hoped she could be as singular, as unique an artist as Exene one day.

Foreign, dark, dusky as some concubine of ancient Abyssinia, Lia went unnoticed. With no clique or companions beside her, she was swept up in a tidal wave of frenzied punk energy, her book of poems leaping from her grasp, the pages falling open, and Lia, before Exene had even completed the band's first song, was crouched down on the ground, pushing at the calves of strangers, coaxing them to lift their combat boots and dirty sneakers off the consecrated verses meant to rescue Ryan.

Though some of them were torn, and most of them smudged with shoeprints, Lia was able to salvage her poems and sketches. From her vantage, somewhere at the midway point of the ballroom, Exene appeared small at the center of the stage, a doll-sized deity emblazoned with rage.

As Exene and John Doe sang the hard, melancholy, and melodic strains of the song, something—the veracity of truth perhaps—caused a blinding light to be turned onto all of them: Lia, Exene and her band— even Ryan, wherever she was. Lia's dream shifted out of its soft, pastel focus, like a fairytale suddenly turned sinister, and right then and there, she realized that she had attempted to take on the impossible. For the past four weeks, she'd willed herself to absorb the blame, fear, and guilt of Ryan's disappearance, and now, as the band cried out in plaintive tones, *"She was still awake..."* Lia felt like a believer in a bankrupt church, and that everything—the fast, haunting harmonies of the band, her own simple and futile earnestness, Ryan's stubborn silence—had conspired against her in one gigantic lie.

She rocked and swayed amidst a sea of sweaty bodies, too dizzy and overwhelmed to search the crowd for black faces and kinky hair; she only knew then that Exene was indeed an angel, no different from any other hovering on some lofty plane, mocking her with the freedom and defiance Lia longed to possess—

a devil angel high on her pedestal stage, likely too self-absorbed or disinterested to ever come to her rescue.

Embarrassed now by their sad, childlike tones, and feeling tired, chagrined, and enraged, Lia claimed the same freedom as the group of guys who slam-danced down at the front of the stage and threw the book of poems to the ground.

Like an arsonist captivated by fire, Lia watched with keen interest as the book was kicked and stomped all throughout the crowd by dancing, oblivious feet.

in a hot-air balloon, in a land far, far away, high above the city, ... a fleeting serenity

LIA PUSHED HER WAY PAST THE WALL OF HARD, SWEATY bodies, through the exit door, and into the crisp San Diego night air, the electric chant, *"blue shock, exchange,"* echoing inside her ears. All it took was a brief sighting of Exene performing onstage to remind Lia of her compelling power as an artist. Lia could envision her then, receiving her earnestly fabricated little book with indifference, or worse yet, scorn. What had she been thinking? Exene was ten times more complex than the stupid kids at school who'd inexplicably bought into her work. Whereas Lia was desperate for some glimmer of hope to cling to, what excuse did those kids have for their blind conviction?

Lia might never get the chance to see X play again. She couldn't be certain if she'd ever see Ryan again either. She retreated from the theater intent upon the water, her heart breaking a tiny little bit with each step.

When Neil strode out of his grandmother's bedroom one morning at the house in Galveston, looking for all the world like a matinee idol, Ryan felt as though she were seeing him for the very first time. His sure-footed swagger was strangely soothing, so that she stopped fretting and missing home, if but for a moment.

He breezed past without a word and went and sat on the small front porch of the little yellow house. Some instinct told her to hang back and let him alone, the way her mother sometimes vacated the living room when her father took over to shout at football players through the TV.

Novia. She recalled only a few words or phrases from Spanish class, preferring to doodle short phrases such as *Ryan & Neil Forever* in bubble letters than give serious attention to the lesson at hand, but *novia*—bride—was one word she remembered well.

Novia. The word rang out like the sacred words muttered over a birthday cake lit full of candles. She remembered the white lace tablecloths that belonged to Grandmother she'd spied one day, kept inside a drawer in the tiny dining room. When no one was around, Ryan scampered to that drawer and retrieved the most intricate, laciest cloth she could find. The visage of herself inside her tiny compact, the tablecloth draped ceremoniously over her head, nearly created the look she envisioned, yet it wasn't quite right. That romantic word would soon describe her, and she didn't have time to waste. She knew it was a twerpy thing to do, but she was the bride, and didn't brides always come first? She began to hack at the tablecloth with a pair of tiny scissors, the only scissors she had, trying to get the veil to fall just so.

The delicate cloth, wrought by the hands of some hardworking, faceless woman in some factory or village somewhere, was a lamb for the slaughter in Ryan's hands. She hacked at the cloth evilly—*"Gol, I'm just a twerp,"* she muttered—in her reckless attempt to right first one side and then the next, until, like a poorly fashioned bob rendered by the hands of a child, the lace was entirely too short and lopsided to function as a veil any longer. She thought of Lia, and the quiet, methodical care she took with her schoolwork and passion projects, such as the book for Exene, and wished she knew how to be still and careful. A sudden pang of longing sprung into her chest, and her heart ached again for home.

She heard voices on the front porch. She cast the ruined white lace to the floor and crept back into the living room, peering to see who it was. "Hey, Dolly, what's shaking?" she heard Neil say, dropping his voice in the way he sometimes did when he thought himself in charge and irrepressibly charming. Even Ryan had to admit, though she was loath to commit the disloyalty of even one bad thought, that he did sound pretty cheesy.

"Ooh, I love that nickname, Neil. So much cuter than Dolores!" the other party said, before deftly switching to Spanish. "*Quer vir conosco?*"

It was a young girl, not a grown-up, with a voice so high and babyish, she fairly emitted a sweetness—the scent of sugar cookies or cotton candy—when she spoke.

Ryan's ears perked. She understood the girl's invitation for Neil to go along with her. But where? And who was she? For some reason, Ryan had an instinct to spy rather than burst through the screen door and show herself. She crouched down on the sofa, peering just above the windowsill.

The girl was impeccably tiny and plump all at once. Whereas Ryan leaned toward chubby, there was no getting around the fullness of Dolores's face, which hovered like a heart-shaped balloon, or her pillowy arms and marshmallow torso. As she walked forward on plump legs and the tiniest of little feet, Ryan noticed a rich, cinnamon complexion that belied her light blond hair—a Mexican girl done up in acts and scenes of makeup and hairspray. Ryan didn't know why, but she breathed deeply then and smiled to herself. With her platinum hair, long, pink frosted nails and swooning lashes, Dolores was a pro who would show her how it was done. Ryan pictured cousin Dolores and all of Neil's sisters circling around her on her grand day, helping her fix her hair and makeup so she'd look just as glamorous, just as much a Texas beauty as each one of them, at her wedding. *I bet Neil would like that.* She giggled then, for no apparent reason. But wasn't that love? Being giddy and suddenly ecstatic for no reason at all?

She could only see him in profile, but the screwhead impression that dimpled his left cheek was unmistakable. Neil wore a big grin as Dolores took the two short front steps up the porch with her doll-sized feet. Neil had to bend quite low to kiss her. Ryan was positively amazed. She could not believe her eyes. After a peck on the lips, they embraced, Dolores on her tiny tippy toes in order to rest her dumpling arms about his neck and shoulders. This girl was no cousin. They kissed again and began to walk slowly, hand in hand, away from Grandmother's porch. Ryan whimpered, too stunned to speak. It seemed to happen so fast and of a sudden, she almost wished it would play out again so she could analyze every nuance and detail to know for certain that everything she'd just seen was *real.* But it was.

Ryan's reckoning came slowly. Was this the 'friend' she'd overheard him speaking to on the phone during her last trip to his apartment in Imperial Beach?

She rushed onto the porch then, trailing Neil as fast as she could. But she had no idea what to say. Tears sprung in place of words, and she stood shivering on the porch, goose bumps rising quickly on her sunburnt arms, frigid in the ninety-degree heat.

Neil marched down the block proudly, displaying Dolores like the most adorable carnival prize a boy could ever hope to win. Just a mere length away from them, Ryan was stunned by just how quickly they seemed to disappear.

Sunshine pierced her eyes, and she cast her gaze downward, making tears drop like water from her fast-melting heart. At her feet, she noticed a straight black line like a strip of electrical tape. Neil had dropped his comb. She gathered it quickly and brought it to her lips in a light kiss, just as she'd seen Grandmother do a handful of times with the rosary she removed from the pocket of her housedress to finger and adore several times a day.

stars clutch sky, weeping

"You ever hear 'The KKK Took My Baby Away'?"
He laughed to himself as he said this, twisting his
mouth to the side in a sinister little chuckle.

These are the words the chubby misfit would speak
later, but first, Lia stood alone, gazing at the darkened
waves.

The water was magnificent, the gorgeous, delicately
undulating waves a terrific substitute for people any
day. If only the world were populated by waves and sea
nymphs, anemones and dolphins—*how wonderful*, she
thought, until she heard footfalls and realized she had
to be alert and streetwise because she was on her own
downtown.

Two men passed behind her, walking closely to
one another and speaking in low voices. There was
something familiar, possibly tender, about the way
the two men interacted, which led Lia to think they

might be homosexuals. Like so much else, she didn't know exactly what it meant to be gay. She only knew that these men sometimes developed deep emotional attachments and sometimes shared apartments and sometimes fell in love.

Besides the occasional passerby, Lia thought that all the time she was all alone and was not frightened to be as long as she could share the company of the quiet, beautiful waves. Yet it wasn't long before she heard a cough, the type of deliberate *"ahem"* made to make the other realize that you are there, from a young man, white, hovering in the shadows, watching the black girl, so new, just minted—a waxen doll fresh off the assembly line.

Lia was not frightened by the guy who approached her with a slow, even pace. He wore jeans and a white oxford shirt open at the collar, a navy windbreaker and black Converse high-tops. He was not a punk. His hair was light brown. His face was smooth, not quite round, but wide and open somehow, like the face of a very young child. To Lia, this man was old, yet in the world, he was fresh-faced, twenty-one if he was a day.

From the very moment he quietly demanded that she notice him, she knew presciently that they would end up talking, and immediately she wondered about his voice, if it would be high-pitched and annoying, or babyish in some way, for there was a sliver of softness hinted at—hidden somewhere in his persona.

The baby-faced man stopped just a foot or two away from her. Too closely. His distance was invasive, not quite socially correct. Still, she did not fear him. In nervousness, she jumped to an enthusiastic confession.

"I went to see X tonight!" She was still beamingly proud of her solitary pilgrimage. Little did this stranger realize how difficult her journey had been. He didn't know Ryan. Or did he? *For it could be him, just as it could be any man, anywhere, responsible for some dark transgression against her.*

"That's pretty rockin'," Baby Face answered dryly. She wondered, did he know X, or was he just pretending to? This mattered to her.

"The concert just got out? It's still kind of early, right?"

His voice, not high, but soft and oddly childlike, suggesting a certain distance—from reality or others, who could say?

"What about The Ramones, you like them? Me, I love 'em."

"You don't look punk." Lia spat out a flat, critical observation somewhat defensively, lest he sneer at her and think the same thing. He did not attack her, this young man who to her seemed much, much older, but lowered his gaze momentarily at the pavement, as though embarrassed by her observation.

Then he asked her about a particular song by The Ramones and laughed to himself, twisting his mouth to the side in a sinister little chuckle. Lia didn't know if he was really amused or if he was simply trying to insult her, payback for saying he didn't look punk, which he might have interpreted as not looking cool. KKK? Was it a racist song? Lia stepped back a bit, wondering if he realized he was standing too close.

"Well, anyway, it's a good song," he continued, his mouth still twisted like the swirls of a candy cane.

"I saw them once—in concert, I mean," Lia muttered, recalling the festival of the previous summer when she and Ryan had spent the day in the sun, dancing to the music of The Ramones.

"Awesome. Anyhow, my name's Chuck. What's yours?"

"Lia," she whispered. For a split second, she'd thought of saying Lisa or Megan.

All the while as they got acquainted, Lia kept inching backward and he kept inching forward, yet Lia knew he didn't mean to give offense.

Lia eyed this man and tried to gauge whether or not he would have been popular at school. She imagined not. His round baby face was both amiable and sad, and Lia could see herself in it, as though his face was a glass which showed her own reflection.

Chuck's preppy clothes were crisp and neat-looking, which helped somehow to redeem his soft, slouchy form and the breath that spread from his small, red-lipped mouth onto her face in a warm christening for which she had not asked.

When Chuck proposed, "Say, you wanna check out that old ship down there?" Lia could barely keep herself from leaping at him with a great yearning, from throwing her arms about his neck and resting her face against his chest. There was something, some secret hidden within the soft fleshy folds that covered the bones of his fingers, in his pudgy belly and saggy trousers, that she suddenly wanted to protect or uncover. Possibly sensing her longing, or feeling it also, he boldly grabbed her hand and began to walk with her toward the eighteenth-century shipping vessel on display along the dock.

She followed him easily, like the bewildered survivor of some catastrophe. It seemed perfectly natural to hold his hand, squeezing the fat of his soft hands as though she was a child playing with a fine ball of fleshy dough. Fused together by the random selection of loneliness, Lia found herself telling Chuck—who she'd learned came from a wealthy family farther up the coast, and had parents who mostly ignored him in favor of his younger sister, and who was happiest driving his showy red sports car down to San Diego, or sometimes even farther down into Mexico, to get inside the complex heart of Tijuana which was seedy and shady and run-down—all about Ryan.

"She's my best friend. I mean, it might not be obvious, but we're like the same person, we have the same thoughts and feelings, and besides, we both love purple, X, Ronnie Spector, and Andy Warhol."

To these declarations Chuck listened carefully, nodding his broad, placid face.

"I mean, we fight sometimes, but that's, like, normal, right? Everyone fights sometimes."

If he was either bored or disinterested in these facts, Chuck did not grow impatient, but continued to hold Lia's hand and stroke her back devotedly.

"But now Ryan's been gone for almost a month, and nobody knows where she is. It's scary. I hate to think it, but like…what if she's dead?"

Lia braced herself to keep her voice from breaking as she spoke. She might have noticed then the mild yet diligent penetration of Chuck's blue eyes, but to Lia, these details were imperceptible in this, a moment of thick, self-indulgent sadness.

"That's too bad about your friend. When I was in tenth grade, I had a classmate who died of leukemia," Chuck offered, his face flat and expressionless.

Lia's throat tightened as she locked away her tears.

It was as though the night was playing itself out in a dream she'd dreamt before. She floated as though in a reverie through a slow-motion, softly lit sequence as they walked to the 7-Eleven. She was not surprised at how easily Chuck became intoxicated on the beer he bought, his dull eyes suddenly glistening with emotion.

"My parents hate me," he muttered. "My dad always says I'm lazy, that I'm not athletic and good-looking like he was at my age. I should probably just shoot myself."

Crouched down in the parking lot on the curb in front of the store, Chuck spoke these words, his small, pink baby mouth pursed into a shape not unlike a tiny rosebud, and Lia felt a snag upon her heart, like a rip in a length of old, rotting fabric, and she lunged toward him, placing her mouth on his, swiftly and with pressure, in the way one might rush to treat a gaping wound. In response, Chuck's mouth was all about hers with the heavy exuberance of a puppy, and Lia felt embarrassed to have this heavyset misfit mauling her with his mouth—and yet, she liked it also.

RS: Well, there's the eye pencil. That's one thing.

EC: I'd hardly say that's reason enough to call a truce. I mean, who doesn't use eye pencil?

RS: Yeah, you're right. Let's record our own version of "Ebony and Ivory." Ha! Aren't I a riot? Hell couldn't freeze fast enough...

EC: So there. We do agree on something.

The collages were one thing, but the girls never spoke directly about the paper dolls—not even to each other. It was just understood: two tow-headed magazine cutouts pasted over Barbie-like bodies. Each of them always played the same role. They never questioned their underlying need for a battle royal; it just always seemed to happen that way.

LIA AND CHUCK ENDED UP SNEAKING INTO THE DANK corridor of an old, decrepit building at some junction of hell, Lia having failed to notice the blank pallet behind his steady gaze. The thin runner of carpet on the floor beneath them in that dirty old building had passed into a stage quite beyond filth, decayed as it was like the dead bones of some old body, fused together now and one with the creaking wooden floor. The hallway smelled of urine and Lia suddenly felt itchy all over.

Her back against the wall in a dark corner of that foul-smelling place, so different, so strange compared to Coronado, Chuck would not let go of her as they stood in a dark corner, rapt in an embrace not of love, until Lia couldn't bear it any longer, until she felt herself suffocating for the smell of the place, the insistence of Chuck prodding and tugging at her, her dress nearly pulled to tearing.

Perhaps Chuck felt her anxiety, because all of a sudden, he dropped down onto the floor dramatically, his mouth wide open, his eyes rolled back into his head; a little boy playing a war game, he pretended for a moment to be dead.

Instantly, Lia awakened to the reality that she was far away from Coronado and that it was getting late and she needed to get home, yet she remained trapped in a fleeting feeling of warmth that confused her. Already having given up the tactile embrace of Chuck's arms, she was still captured by the grip of defiance. Suddenly, the sting of her suppressed injuries intensified, and in words, Karen Green rushed toward her: "*Don't think for a minute you have me fooled. Whatever Ryan does, you do. You're as thick as thieves.*" And she wondered if Karen Green was right.

Feeling that Karen's words had been some sort of prophecy, she wanted to lunge toward Chuck, to finish what she started, to live with and through Ryan at such a bleak and ignorant distance she could scarcely recall anymore which one of them had vanished.

Looking over at Chuck, she saw it again: the flat, inexpressive look in his eyes, and that smirk which belied his soft hands and tender phrases, a look of humored self-satisfaction twisted onto his face—and she knew then that she had come full circle, that she had arrived at the same junction through which she had passed before and thus was still lost.

If Ryan had Neil, she would have Chuck, just like Karen said. Whatever Ryan does, you do. "Chuck, let's go. It reeks in here."

Chuck only stood and dusted himself off, tugging and rearranging his clothing with a satisfied nonchalance.

"I'm sorry," he said finally. "I don't think I've enough gas to make it across the bridge and back to take you home."

"But you promised..." Lia insisted. "What am I going to do now? The last bus ran thirty minutes ago!"

Lia knew she was utterly doomed, but she postponed her reaction, choking back tears simply because she was sick and tired of being a sad sack. Too chagrined and terrified to cry openly, she could only stand there in shocked silence, wondering how her paramour of loneliness had already begun to retreat so swiftly from her grasp. For a moment, with a pain coursing through her and a salt blood taste in her mouth, Lia realized that she could never be lost like Ryan. No matter which man might abduct her (*What was it like? The wonder! Desired enough for a kidnapping!*), if she were taken away she would only make a shallow grave and premature bones—a brief article in the newspaper perhaps. No matter what, she would always be the token, dimple-smiled black girl—in much the same way that one penny is for good luck, whereas an entire bucketful is hardly worth counting.

"...like a woman"
Universal Corner, X

Lia rushed outside, leaving Chuck and the thick, putrid air of that dirty old building. Her body scratched all over, attacked by a feral boy (yet another sacrifice for Ryan, she thought, to help save her). Oh, how she longed then for a boy like Jody. A boy smart enough to place her at the center of the frame, a longing so deep and acute she had to block the thought of it entirely, for the reminder of what she'd lost, of what Ryan had forced her to give up, nearly brought her undone.

Home. Suddenly after her night alone (no matter who she'd met, all along she'd been terribly alone), the saccharine comfort of her bed seemed like a quaint yet not entirely unpleasant notion. But how to get there? She was so lost, so confused inside her mind, she had no idea how to get home. Chuck had promised to take her, but he had abandoned her, breaking his promise. She realized then, in useless retrospect, that she should have paid closer attention to the matte, gray flatness behind his eyes when he spoke to her.

The buses had long stopped running. In the immediate absence of water, she relied upon the air to cleanse her, yet she was so frightened, and too proud to admit to herself just how crushed she was by Chuck's cold, flat abandonment.

She crept now from the shadow of one building to the next. The streets were deserted. Eerily quiet. Where were all the kids who'd gone to see X? She had turned her back on them all: John Doe, Exene, all those kids at the concert. How she longed for them now—so desperately.

charismatic painting weeps tears of blood

AT THE END OF A DESOLATE BLOCK UP A HILL (WHEREAS Coronado was flat, neat, a lovely island at sea, San Diego had so many hills), there seemed to be life. After a flurry of swift steps, she reached it; a lighted oasis, a blinking sign above the entrance cried Cold Draft Beer! She peered inside, squinting into the darkly tinted brown glass; a sprinkling of men sat at a bar altogether, and yet their aura suggested a loneliness deeper than anything Lia could imagine.

Presently, a young man swung open the barroom door and staggered out into the street. Her first instinct being protection, she ducked behind a metal newspaper dispenser not yet filled with Sunday's *San Diego Union Tribune*. Would there be any word about Ryan in there the next day?

The man who'd left the bar seemed young, narrow-shouldered. He wore a beige windbreaker and had sandy blond hair. The sailor Keith! Suddenly she felt a desperate pang of love searing her veins, only to explode inside her heart. She'd been wrong. She should have taken him more seriously. He'd been so kind to her. He could have been her secret; a paramour of kindness, forever adrift at sea.

Imperceptibly, like a secret whispered to herself, Lia began to trace the footsteps of this young man. It was him, wasn't it, the sailor Keith? All she needed was to call his name and he'd turn to her, just as gently as ever. *"My darling, how I've missed you,"* he'd say. Or perhaps he wasn't the sailor Keith at all, but a ghost, a marauding pirate usurping his identity.

For four blocks, Lia danced with this young man. She followed at a pace near enough to see him. All the time, she kept him keen within her sight like a hawk eyeing her prey, and yet she kept her footfalls quiet. She became a stealthy black cat, stalking loneliness, ready to fight it, to stab it dead in the midst of an abandoned, nighttime street.

When the young, beige-jacketed man paused to allow a lone car to barrel through the wide, empty street, Lia also halted a few paces behind him, shrinking into the embrace of shadows. Where was he going? Sooner or later, she'd have to stop and find her own way. Yet she was counting on him, a beacon star, to keep her from being alone. They were two strangers separated by a pace, a distance of some yards, yet in his shadow, she was not alone.

Suddenly, in that instantaneous spark that ignites a fire, or an unexpected spate of cold water falling overhead—from whatever perspective you considered it, it came to Lia swiftly—the man, not quite as young as he'd initially seemed, quickly turned to face her, hollering at her in a sharp, nasal tone.

"Hey! You following me, girl?"

Lia stuttered with her eyelashes, blinking rapidly; they told how she was stunned. How had he seen her? And his voice, like the man with dramatic ways who used to work in the school cafeteria. Tacking 'girl' on the end, like somebody's black grandma at the stove with a hand on her hip.

"You got your friends hiding somewhere, ready to come out and jump me? I've been jumped by niggers before, but not this time. Tell your friends this white boy hasn't got any cash on him, but he does have a gun. Now, fuck off, little girl."

Lia froze in her tracks, speechless, shattered, but why? She stood so still, her tongue deadened like ice. How to tell it? How to explain that she wished to take nothing—only to offer an available, insatiable heart.

Coming into Coronado over the Bay Bridge, Ryan and Neil felt dazed, for only then could they perceive the magnitude of their effrontery against Ryan's parents, the authorities, her friends—even Cindy and little Craig. Ryan was too bewildered, too lost to even realize she was returning on the very day she and Lia had marked on their calendars two months before: the day X was set to play over in San Diego.

In the final mile before Ryan's house, Neil nudged the car forward at the pace of a hearse leading a funeral procession, and indeed they were dead, hovering as they were like gloomy spirits over the corpse of their mortal passion.

Having abandoned their initial plans for an adolescent wedding, the reason for their prodigal return was not because they'd been too consumed with one another to abandon some Tijuana conjugal bed, but because Neil had convinced Ryan to stay on with him in Galveston until his father returned, and then after that, hedging fresh bets, Neil insisted she stay on in seclusion so that he could spend some time with his dad before heading back to Cali and dealing with the fallout of having stolen away with her in the first place.

As they moved along the curves of the towering bridge, Ryan and Neil paid the price for the ruse they created, for once trapped inside a dungeon of lies; they had no idea how to plot their escape, to stand in the sunshine of truth without getting burned.

With a new father who was sometimes drunk and sometimes sober, and always calm and placid in his demeanor, Neil found himself a sugar substitute and was unable to reciprocate Ryan's surplus devotion. Initially, she'd made a concerted effort to understudy her future role as Mrs. Jimenez, helping Neil's grandmother chop vegetables and bathe her Pomeranian Millie in the kitchen sink. But inevitably, no matter how hard she tried, she faced moments of panic. Draping her arms over Neil's shoulders, she mewed.

"Are we ever getting married? I'm missing a lot of school, you know. What if I get held back next year? I don't want to graduate when I'm, like, twenty."

From the very start, Neil's grandmother had been suspicious.

"She looks pretty young. Shouldn't she be in school?"

"Nah, she's homeschooled. Her parents are total hippies. They spend half the day high on weed. Besides, her parents are glad she's making the trip; they believe in the educational benefit of travel."

Grandmother considered Neil with an arch expression, yet she decided to go easy on this new grandson with whom she had only just become acquainted because she was sympathetic to his obvious frailties. Sagacious with the wisdom of years, what harm would a few days of missed lessons do Ryan in the long run, she reasoned? She felt for these modern kids, whose parents were almost just as adolescent as they were, smoking pot at home and permitting all sorts of leniencies. If anything, Grandmother liked the idea of keeping the kids with her for a while—perhaps she could set some sort of straightening rod against Neil's crooked spine, all while keeping him close beneath the shelter of her protective wing.

Yet, when Grandmother realized that Neil was too captivated by his drunken father to heed her subtle directives, and the days had begun to drag on and turn into weeks, she began to nudge the kids—two amnesiac homing pigeons who'd seemingly lost their way—back in the direction of home. "I think I'll move you kids into the house out back."

The "house out back" was a small shed in the yard behind the main house where Neil's father sometimes slept. Cleverly, Grandmother knew the kids wouldn't last long cramped into that little house like chickens too constricted to peck their way around a coop.

In the modest quarters of the backyard shed, Ryan became the aberration that Lia had seen perched on the edge of her bed at dawn. In vacant daylight, Ryan stretched her outsize frame on the sleeping bag Neil's grandmother had put down on the floor for her. Listless as a mermaid, Ryan plucked her brows into fine arches, stained her lips with cherry gloss, and creamed her cuticles for hours on end.

Neil swooned daily, full to bursting with feelings that ranged from the serendipity of new love to a simmering aversion for his father. He was soothed by the lullaby of the stories his father told him of his days as a young man.

"I had moves, man. You should have seen me on the dance floor. More epic than James Brown...I'm talking smooth. Your grandma used to have to take the phone off the hook to get any sleep, so many girls were calling." Yet Neil was equally repulsed by the sound of his slurred speech and retching out on the lawn each morning.

All-consumed as he was by the fresh fervor of love, for Neil too, Ryan became an ethereal flesh-ghost who was no longer able to penetrate his desperate obsession with the inscrutable man who was his father. Each night, fighting the confines of irrelevancy, Ryan twirled the frayed ends of her hair around a curling iron and tried to look hopeful as she offered to fetch the men a snack.

A glimpse of herself in the glass is what brought Ryan to a reckoning. Preening in a handheld mirror had failed to capture the entire picture, like the big patches of brown hair that had mushroomed around her scalp, the dark circles beneath her eyes that made her look like she had her mother's face, and her fat—in the weeks since they'd been away, the fat from her face had retreated, making her, compared to her old self, appear gaunt and hollow-cheeked as though she were ill.

Seeing herself like this, Ryan realized that her Jane Mansfield curves were being ironed straight, and that her dimples didn't have enough fat in which to poke themselves. She barely recognized herself. She was losing sight of her identity, and she suddenly felt terrible guilt for going ahead with life behind her parents' back. Forced to confront the purposeful betrayal that she and Neil had perpetrated, all of a sudden it seemed absurd that she had deliberately lied, and that her family and Lia didn't know where she was, and at once she was so guilty she felt mean inside, as though her heart had been moved not by love, but by a sort of depraved, aimless narcissism. She began to weep mournfully and tried to pack her things through bleary eyes, all while cursing Baudelaire under her breath.

It just so happened that Grandmother's fury coincided with Ryan's tears, because she came out to the little spare house then, rapping at the door with aged knuckles. Having made a connection—together with Ryan's parents, Neil's mother finally suspected that Neil had done the unthinkable, that he'd actually sought out the father who he'd always petulantly pretended to hate, and together the two mothers had huddled with nothing but tears, hope, prayer, and *bingo!*—Grandmother confirmed that they had indeed been partaking of her handmade tamales and suspicious glances for more than two weeks.

"You lied to me, Neil!" Spittle flew from the corners of Grandmother's mouth she was so enraged. "You told me her parents knew where she was. Do you realize her mother is crazy with worry? You have to take her home right now, or else the police will come, and I don't want trouble."

Caught red-handed in stealth possession of a jilted teenage bride, Neil began to stammer. Grandmother didn't understand his blueprint, how he had needed Ryan to guide him to her door, that without her their lives might have passed like two stars shooting in opposite directions in a dark sky.

"It's not what you think. We were gonna tell you— everybody. We just needed some time. We were gonna get married. Or maybe we'd wait, get our own place here, and Ryan would start school again, and I'd sign on as her legal guardian."

As Neil flooded his grandmother's ears with his rambling explanation, he realized that he in fact had had no plan, only a fatal thirst that would have killed him had it not been sated in time.

Grandmother only shook her head, her eyes wet with tears. "For years you were lost to us, Neily. We never had a chance to know you. I know what it is to survive each day, a misplaced child haunting your heart. Why didn't you just tell us your problems so we could help you? We love you, son. You never have to lie to us."

For so long, family for Neil had consisted of two half-sisters and a mom. He never could have anticipated the weight, the responsibilities that came with the unconditional love rushing from the heart of these kindred strangers. On hearing Grandmother's scolding reprimand and soothing reassurances both, Neil only wanted to fall to his knees and bury his head in her lap, to weep at the loss of the days and hours that made her measure of love more foreign to him than the rapid Spanish she wove with her sharp yet honeyed tongue, which he could not understand.

As Neil guided the Camaro back through the space he and Ryan had traversed only weeks before, oblivious to the endless pool of desert that lay vast and matter of fact on either side of the roadway, he felt the heaviness of shame bend his shoulders. Before the eyes of a grandmother he had only freshly grown to love, and a father teetering indecisively between drunkenness and sobriety, all Neil could see was his own failure.

Crowning Ryan with the scepter of his shame and devastation, he berated her for the duration of the trip.

"I knew it. Damn, I just knew it!" Neil slammed his open palm against the steering wheel until it stung. "I should have sent you home after the first week. All you did was get in the way. On your butt, painting your nails and screwing around with sticky lip gloss. I didn't need you to stay. I could have dealt with all this on my own."

Ryan hadn't the strength to broker a defense, but only toppled down, imploding in a mess unto herself. She sobbed behind a Kleenex and dabbed at her eyes, knowing it was all wrong—and that was and had always been the point—to flaunt her rebellion in the face of everyone too scared to step outside the pre-drafted boundaries of right and wrong, to live a real-life adventure beyond the confines of popularity rules that automatically counted her among the rejects.

Tears cut at Neil's eyes as he damned her over and over again, and Ryan was utterly stunned by the revelation that every notion she'd ever had of love, in reality, was not at all what she had thought.

Palms smeared bloody

AFTER HER SCOLDING AT THE HANDS OF THE YOUNG, beige jacketed man, Lia stooped onto a curb, too fearful to move forward or retrace her steps. She decided she would simply stay put until death or daylight arrived to claim her.

A police car pulled up alongside her, and two cops asked why she was out alone so late at night. It was 5 a.m. and dawn was on the horizon. They coaxed her inside the patrol car, amused by her wariness of them, as she was obviously fearful that they might hurt her. Before crossing back over the bridge to Coronado, where they would safely deposit her home, the two cops—one white, one black, both middle-aged, their tummies burdened by the girth of fast food diets—doted on her like two uncles. After stopping at some twenty-four-hour doughnut place, they'd come out carrying a cup of hot chocolate for her, and a cake donut dusted with powdered sugar, which the white cop thrust at her through the open car window.

Lia sipped the cocoa timidly, not trusting that it was not laced with some drug. With the same reluctance, she took a small bite of doughnut. Sugar caused a wave of nausea to rush through her system. The dinner her mother had forced her to eat so many hours before still cowered inside her. Now, it came rushing to the fore. Releasing fear, exhaustion, anger, vomit splattered all along the back seat of the patrol car as the officers pulled up to the pewter-colored house on Palm Avenue. Too ashamed to apologize, Lia wiped her mouth with the back of her hand, ducked quietly out of the car, and scampered inside.

IN HER NIGHT OF EPIC WANDERING, LIA HAD BEEN forgetful of all else but love—*Vainly do I try to find the wound*—so that she didn't even realize that she'd staged a Ryanesque reenactment of unbearable worry for her parents.

The phone rang at the Payne home at 2 a.m.

"Dear God, no!" Dorothea shrieked as she and her husband lay in bed wide awake, their eyes flung toward the ceiling in darkness—two fresh cadavers, not yet cold inside their coffins, waiting for the reality of death to sink in.

"Calm down," Greg Payne scolded. "It's probably Lia calling for a ride."

Greg picked up the phone after just one ring. Listening intently, he drew in a quick breath. Mrs. Payne sat bolt upright, a marionette tugged by a string at the top of her head. She saw worry on her husband's face. She could tell it wasn't Lia calling. Dorothea watched, feeling helpless as the corners of her husband's mouth collapsed into a frown.

"My God, when?" My God, he kept saying. Suddenly, tears wet his eyes. Dorothea gasped.

"Just a moment, please." Greg Payne placed his hand over the receiver and spoke to his wife. Shaking his head, he told her, "It's not what you think. It's Karen. Ryan—they've found her. She's okay!"

Mrs. Payne sighed deeply. Greg put down the phone. "Thank God. Jesus. What a relief, she's home safe. Thank God that's over with."

The Paynes spent little time speculating on what had happened. Who'd abducted Ryan? Where he'd taken her? Or was it willful? Had all along Ryan been just another teenage runaway? Karen Green hadn't offered many details and Greg Payne knew it wasn't the time to ask. Neither had he wanted to spoil Karen Green's moment of triumph by mentioning that, now, their daughter (perennially good, trustworthy, a keeper of promises and rules) was officially late by four hours. Besides, how could four hours compare to four weeks of blind ignorance about a daughter—not knowing if she were alive or dead?

Relieved though they were about Ryan, the Paynes felt themselves lurching into yet another unknowable spate of terror, a rollercoaster ride not programmed to stop. It was Dorothea Payne who'd finally thrown back the bedsheet and marched over to the phone, dialing the San Diego police in a fury.

"What are you doing?" Greg Payne had bellowed. Relishing the comfort of fatalism, he preferred to wait, unwilling to entertain the notion that anything untoward could have happened.

"Calling the police in San Diego. To hell with these idiots in Coronado."

Within forty minutes of Mrs. Payne's phone call, the police found Lia. In one night, both girls were returned (though no one would ever know that for six hours, Lia had roamed the streets of San Diego on a love quest). As soon as she came in the house, Lia was greeted by the faces of her parents, still stricken with worry and also relief, because finally the entire ordeal was over. They could go back to being themselves: regular parents, no longer tiptoeing around their daughter as though she might break.

It would be years before Lia could actually laugh at the fact that Ryan had upstaged her—pulling up in front of her parents' home in Neil Jimenez's car, leaping from the passenger seat at 1 a.m., and racing across the lawn to beat on her parents' front door with her fists, her hair hanging down her back tangled, brown, and greasy.

When she did emerge, tumbling out of the Camaro that Saturday (having missed X by only a few hours), it never was clear to anyone outside the Greens' immediate family whether Ryan had left of her own accord—a saucy child bride, hair whipping around her face from the open car window while Neil gunned the engine in a race to get to Mexico—or if she'd been coerced and taken against her will. Some members of the community noted, however, that a sheriff's car sat parked outside the Green home for at least an hour that night, and that the sheriff and a deputy were spotted entering and retreating from the house.

Neil was ultimately charged with misdemeanor child endangerment. He did not contest the charges, but willfully turned himself into the Coronado police. He was sentenced to three months of house arrest, and through it all, Lia marveled, enviously imagining how terrific it all must have been.

an Ophelia resuscitated, revived

Two weeks after she'd come back to Coronado, Lia caught a glimpse of Ryan through the glass of Karen Green's car window in the parking lot of the Safeway. Ryan had seemed deader then, through that window, than Lia could ever have imagined. Not her face, but a face that looked very much like hers—only paler, narrower, and terribly frightened—had hovered behind the window of that car.

With Ryan's newfound celebrity, Lia was almost thrilled at having spotted her. Once her closest confidant, Ryan had retreated behind a shroud of tight security like an impossibly inaccessible superstar. Yet, for a fleeting instant, she had been almost close enough to touch.

Ryan had lost weight. She no longer appeared older—a knowing Mamie Van Doren with acne—but looked almost normal, like a regular teenage girl. The gossip around school was that her parents had bought her a breast reduction to help her recover from the whole ordeal, which she refused to ever discuss. Ryan's fair skin was baby-powder pale, and she'd had a haircut, and she seemed, with her sick, frail-looking demeanor, more beautiful than ever before, all as though she'd only just returned from a spa, or an adolescent fat farm, and not the putative badlands of Neil Jimenez's wavering heart.

Beyond the Valley
of the Dolls

RYAN HAD SEEN LIA IN THE PARKING LOT OF THE Safeway and had longed to get out the car and call, "Hey Lia, wait up," but shame and fear had kept her motionless behind the safety of tinted glass.

Having been born with the preternatural look of a woman in disgrace had been punishment enough, so that Ryan never imagined that Neil would have outwitted her or done her a bad turn, or that her lark would have ended so disastrously. Her plan of returning to Coronado, brazen and triumphant, to show them all—Elizabeth Cole, Lia, Megan Hamilton—what real love really looked like, had been one appalling fiasco. Chastened by the error of her ways, Ryan dressed modestly, lightened her makeup, and spent most of her time indoors, pining away for a normal boy her own age, and remembering wistfully her days, now seemingly an era long past, with Lia.

The only time Lia seemed accessible again, as though Ryan might actually call to say '*hi*,' or plan a trip into the city, was at nighttime. In dreams, Lia floated over her head, a gingerbread angel, dusting Ryan all over with talc and a whisper of mild words. *"Slow down, Ryan; time moves in circles."* In these sequences, Ryan became the serene cadaver Lia had imagined when she'd first learned the news of her disappearance, so that Ryan looked down on herself in that cold, stony, and quixotic mausoleum, freshly reliving the anguish of her family and friends over and over again, until she was powerless to do anything but clutch her pillow and sob grand, choking sobs.

SOMEHOW, THOUGH IT WAS NEVER SPOKEN ALOUD, Ryan's feelings of shame (at both herself and her brother for what he had done to Lia) and Lia's foolhardy, mawkish devotion had been too great an embarrassment for either of them to live down.

Harlequin

THE FILM REEL IS NEARING ITS END. THERE ARE JUST A few frames of grainy black-and-white footage left, and it appears Exene is making her final appearance as Ryan, and that Ryan in turn is impersonating Exene.

In a spacious loft area on the top floor of some building in San Diego, Exene moves gracefully in soft light. Her trademark scowl erased, her face is calm, naturally serene. She wears an old-fashioned navy dress with white polka dots and a sailor collar, and black-and-white saddle shoes with little white socks.

Lia has carefully torn out the sheets of the journal she never managed to present and has pasted each page along the wall of that sparse, sunlit space. Exene tours the room like a society lady at a gallery, carefully taking in the work. Lia observes her with mean eyes and a sulking mouth, prepared for harsh words, ready to jump to her own defense.

Exene utters no word, but only offers a delicate nod every so often that could mean approval. This sets Lia into a fury, so that she rushes about the room, tearing down the pictures and poems, shredding them in her hands.

EPILOGUE

Hey Lia,
Thanks for the book. I've never heard of Maya
Angelou before but I will give it a try.
XO,
Ryan

The girls were too romantic to be cut and dry at the demise of their friendship. In an unclaimed locker in a quiet corridor of the high school, one of them—which one, what matter? Even in the face of the fatality of their bond, the girls remained fused together so that it was still impossible at times for them to recall who had done what—had started a shrine. One of the girls had pasted the tiny paper doll cutout of Exene, which captured her usual, smoldering defiance, atop a portion of painted gilt cardboard and tacked it up on the back wall of the locker.

For a time, the locker became a timeless portal, a safe place for the girls to have a meeting of minds. One of the two of them might leave a poem, a bottle of some new nail polish, or the name of a new band— though how could anything be better—absurd, the very notion—than X?

In the neutral zone of the abandoned locker, Ryan became what she'd never been before: a normal teenage girl, de-womanized, girlish, coy. In the era B.N. (*before Neil*), it was as though she'd been ten, suddenly thirteen, then careering madly toward forty—a buxom, worldly dame, but only in appearance, *never inside herself*. Never mind about moments of precocious willfulness when she pantomimed adulthood—lacy drawers, pilfered cigarettes, and trash books don't make anyone grown. Yet here, in a space that would begin as a shrine to Exene and become something else entirely, Ryan could show her face, begin to remove the stain of her experience with Neil, and be tender still.

Ryan found a place where she could be sweet to her former best friend without the complications of rivalry, jealousy, and the uneven pacing of their former preoccupations, the hunger of a wayward woman-child juxtaposed against the fears of a girl still held fast inside the arms of innocence.

The girls mostly liked to leave sweet, feminine things for one another, as though they still spent lazy afternoons sprawled on Ryan's bed, reading their horoscopes and giving one another manicures.

Hi Lia, here's a recipe for a homemade facial made
with cucumber and honey.
Love, Ryan

Above the notes, tattered copies of *Cosmo*, or books
by authors like Angelou, Didion, or Borges that Lia had
freshly discovered, Exene stared out at them, her face
framed by the hastily fashioned gilt frame—yet she was
somehow diminished, as the role she'd played in their
lives had already begun to wane. Exene, their once-and-
forever thrall, hovered inside the shrine, festooned
with dried flowers, locks of hair tied with ribbons (Ryan
had carefully wound one thin, pale blue ribbon around
a lock of Neil's black hair, as both a sobering note of
caution and something of a joke), half-burned candles,
and photos of Ryan and Lia—when being together had
been the easiest, most natural thing in the world.

In the weeks following Ryan's return, the girls
tracked their history with an increasing fervor, an
indication that indeed there was no turning back, no
chance of reconciling their friendship. It was as though
they feared they might forget their most cherished
memories if they failed to record them with care.
Thus, they even went as far as to put up photos of
themselves in the third and fourth grade, before they'd
ever known one another, to mark like a height chart
the increasingly steep and challenging incline from
childhood to adolescence, and from adolescence to
that most frightening, obscure thing they were fast
approaching.

In the end, Ryan was the last to write.

Dear Lia, I made you a new paper doll of Ronnie Spector, just for fun…Didn't the one you had before end up falling apart or something? I found the photo in Rolling Stone. I thought you did your eye makeup kind of like this the last time we went to see X play. Whenever I see a picture of her, I think of you. Anyway, I met this new guy, his name is Kyle. Can't write any more now, gotta get ready for my date!
Later, Ryan. xo

Lia palmed the photo of Ronnie Spector, a feeling of taut, bemused anger swelling inside her as she regarded it. Sure, she loved Ronnie Spector—she adored her strong, timeless, bad-girl voice. And there was something about her heavy makeup and elaborate hairdressing that suggested the dreamy, captivating glamour of another era. Beyond that, Lia was angry, finally recognizing the shape of things so long after the fact. All along, Lia had been the one to really take X seriously, to honor Exene and the band with her own fledgling talents. Whereas Ryan had easily cast it all aside, and for what? The temporal warmth of Neil's seductive, yet fleeting affections. Now, here was Ryan, telling her, indirectly, that Ronnie Spector was a more appropriate muse for her, the star black girl out of a total of three in all of Coronado High.

In an instant, everything came back to Lia in a wash of putrid green and yellow, searing memories burning at her skin like an acid: from the abuse she'd suffered at the hands of Jeff Green, to the infuriating nasal tone of the beige-jacketed man and the cruel words he'd hollered at her in the middle of the nighttime street, and even her tolerance of Ryan, and of herself and her easy abandonment of her budding friendship with Jody, all because his attentions toward her had made Ryan mad. Now look where her fervid, mauling devotion had led—to the arms of Chuck in a filthy apartment building she might never have entered, for it was just such a filthy tenement, pitched in a black ghetto somewhere, that her parents had worked so hard to spare her in the first place.

Lia cupped the tiny cutout of Ronnie Spector, gazing at it deliberately; the singer's hooded doe eyes, heavy in their liquid eyeliner and false lashes, reminded Lia of her own ever-trusting, ever-hopeful eyes. Lia balled the photo into a tight wad, crushing Ronnie's romantic gaze, and with it, she hoped to crush every sliver of her own miserable naïveté and the little tremors of social truth that had shaken her for so long, like boys who don't ask you to dance or nobody in the entire school uses *Afro Sheen* but you.

With anger making her movements jerky yet swift, Lia reached into the locker and tore down the paper doll Exene. She would take it home and paste it inside her journal. She threw the crumpled photo of Ronnie Spector in a nearby wastepaper basket and stomped off down the hall, singing, *"the world's a mess, it's in my kiss"* as she went.

author's acknowledgments

I EXTEND MY DEEPEST THANKS TO VANESSA Willoughby for her keen editorial insight and championship of my work, and to Mary Ann Rivers and Ruthie Knox for their ingenuity, patience, and kind support! I'm very proud to have my dear friend Crystal White's artistic excellence grace the cover. A big thank-you also goes to Amina Cain and Itiyopiya Ewart for their early reads of the book, and to Nikki Giovanni and Kwame Alexander for their radiant kindness and generosity. Innumerable thanks to my parents, Raymond and Beverly Collins, my brother Steve, cousin Victor, and all the other scintillating stars in my orbit who I have the privilege to call friends.

about the author

Camille Collins has an MFA in creative writing from The School of the Art Institute of Chicago. She has been the recipient of the Short Fiction Prize from the South Carolina Arts Commission, and her writing has appeared in *The Twisted Vine*, a literary journal of Western New Mexico University. She likes writing about music and has contributed features and reviews to Afropunk and *BUST*. She lives in New York City.

CPSIA information can be obtained
at www.ICGtesting.com
Printed in the USA
BVHW04s2306180918
527859BV00016B/83/P

9 781948 559058